Nicola Marsh is a
multi-award-winni
than losing herself
a previous life, she now divides
raising two dashing heroes, whipping up delish meals,
cheering on her footy team and writing—her dream
job. And she chats on social media. A lot. Come say
hi! Instagram, Twitter, Facebook—she's there! Also
find her at nicolamarsh.com

If you liked *Sweet Thing*, why not try

My Royal Temptation by Riley Pine
Make Me Want by Katee Robert
Ruined by Jackie Ashenden

Discover more at millsandboon.co.uk

SWEET THING

NICOLA MARSH

MILLS & BOON

First Published in Great Britain 2018
by Mills & Boon, an imprint of HarperCollins*Publishers*
1 London Bridge Street, London, SE1 9GF

© 2018 Nicola Marsh

ISBN: 978-0-263-93208-9

MIX
Paper from
responsible sources
FSC® C007454

This book is produced from independently certified FSC™ paper
to ensure responsible forest management.
For more information visit www.harpercollins.co.uk/green.

Printed and bound in Spain
by CPI, Barcelona

This one's dedicated to Flo Nicoll and Nicola Caws,

two of the best editors a girl could wish for.

Thanks for your enthusiasm, your support and your all-round awesomeness.

You rock!

CHAPTER ONE

Abby

D-DAY SHOULD'VE BEEN the happiest day of my life.

I'd envisaged a fabulous eight hours at Le Miel, creating the French pastries I'd grown to adore over the last year, followed by an intimate evening with a bottle of Shiraz and Channing Tatum.

What better way to celebrate a divorce than with a rich red to tantalise my palate and a hot guy strutting across my TV screen?

But my dreams of drooling into my wineglass over Channing turned to crap about an hour into the working day, when Remy King, the best boss in Australia, took a tumble off a ladder and ended up here, in Sydney Private Hospital.

'You don't need to stay,' he said, his blue eyes filled with pain despite being dosed up on enough painkillers to fell an elephant. 'Go back to the shop.'

'Makayla has it covered.' I perched delicately on the edge of his bed and reached for his hand. 'Besides, I finished making the croissants, beignets, éclairs and macarons before you decided to do your lousy circus impression, so there's not much left for her to do but serve.'

He managed a wan smile and winced. 'It was the ladder's fault.'

'Yeah, it just happened to move sideways on that patch of flour on the floor all by itself.' I rolled my eyes. 'If you weren't such a great boss and friend, I'd give you an ass-kicking for being so stupid.'

'And if you weren't the best apprentice I've ever had, I'd sack you on the spot for being so bold.'

I squeezed his hand, thanking God every day that this man had given me a chance when I needed it most.

Apparently leaving my cold, calculating husband after only nine months of marriage 'wasn't the done thing' in the Prendigast family.

Not that my parents had cared why I'd done it. All they'd worried about was their precious reputation as one of the wealthiest families in Sydney, so they had cut me off financially and emotionally to teach me a lesson.

They'd expected me to come running back to their harbourside mansion in the first week.

I hadn't been back in a year.

Yet for all their faults, I missed my folks. My friends too. But I'd left Abigail Prendigast, the perfect daughter in a perfect world who did exactly as she was told, behind that fateful day I'd walked out on my old life and into my new.

'What's wrong?' Remy's eyes narrowed, studying me. 'If it's the patisserie, don't worry, you don't have to handle the place on your own. I've already contacted Tanner, and he'll be happy to help run the place while I'm recuperating.'

I stiffened. While I'd never met Remy's younger brother, I'd heard enough to form an impression. And it wasn't good.

The guy sounded like a flake. A rich flake, who ran nightclubs and bars along the eastern seaboard, made a squillion from them, but spent most of his time flitting overseas squandering his fortune on women.

Yet for some reason Remy seemed to adore him. I'd heard genuine emotion in his voice every time Tanner called from one of his far-flung destinations. Guess I had to give the guy credit for keeping in touch with his brother despite his playboy lifestyle.

I'd seen him once too, while Remy had been chatting to him on a teleconference call. It had been a fleeting glimpse of dark hair, dark eyes and stubble-covered jaw. Handsome if you liked that kind of thing. Me? I preferred uncomplicated, the opposite of Bardley, my ex, and the glower I'd seen on Tanner was enough to tell me he had complication all over him.

'Isn't Tanner overseas?' I asked, sounding way calmer than I felt. I didn't need some stranger who wouldn't know a praline from a peach melba looking over my shoulder. I was confident in my work at Le Miel and didn't need some rich-boy novice slowing me down. 'Because I can handle the everyday running on my own.'

'You can't create and do everything else.' Concern clouded his gaze before he blinked, and I wondered if I'd imagined it. 'Tanner is a great businessman. He's run restaurants. He'll handle things at Le Miel for a month before I'm back on deck.'

'A *month*?' It came out a yell, and Remy chuckled.

'That's what the doc said. Apparently the more I keep off the fractured ankle and rest up the broken ribs, the faster it'll all heal.' He winked. 'Who knew?'

Damn, I should've known he couldn't use crutches to move around the shop when he had three broken ribs too. But when he'd said Tanner would be overseeing the daily operations, I'd envisaged a week, tops. Now I'd have to put up with the gypsy playboy for a month?

Feeling guilty for my selfishness when my friend was in pain, I squeezed his hand again. 'You focus on healing fast. I'll take care of the rest.'

'Don't you mean *we*?'

A deep voice came from behind me, the kind of voice that invoked images of dark bars, dark chocolate and dark souls. Deep. Rich. With an underlying hint of impudence that immediately put me on guard.

I turned and locked gazes with the devil himself.

Crap. Those eyes. A startling sienna, almost golden, the brown was so light. But it wasn't the colour that unnerved me as much as the way they looked at me.

Like I was a tasty *tarte tatin* waiting to be devoured.

An involuntary shiver crept down my spine as that hungry stare zeroed in on my hand, where it lay covering Remy's on the bed.

'Isn't this cosy?' His insolent drawl made me bristle. 'Hope I'm not interrupting anything?'

I snatched my hand away as Remy said, 'Don't be a dick. Tanner, this is Abby, my apprentice and the best damn French pastry chef outside of Paris.'

'Next to you, of course, bro.' Tanner's assessing

gaze focussed on me and damn if the parts of me that hadn't experienced a guy's touch in over a year didn't zing. In a big way.

'That goes without saying.' Remy beamed, his affection obvious as he beckoned Tanner closer. 'Thanks for doing this.'

'My pleasure.' As Tanner stepped forward, I stood and resisted the urge to scoot away.

As if those eyes weren't enough, the closer he got I realised how big the guy was. Huge. At least six-three, with the kind of build honed from many hours in a gym. Or doing other forms of exercise.

Hell. Where had that come from? For the second time in less than a minute, I'd associated sex with him.

I really needed a bout between the sheets. If I could ever be bothered.

Being celibate since Bardley hadn't been an issue. I'd been too busy assembling a life that didn't involve society high teas, expensive dinners to woo clients and yachting on the weekends. All this squeezed around my business degree. Which I'd also walked away from. Bully for me.

'Actually, your timing couldn't be better.' Tanner dwarfed everything in the room as he propped against the bed. 'I've been looking for a new challenge.'

My skin prickled with awareness as Tanner's daring stare alerted me to the fact he wasn't just talking about Le Miel.

Either Remy was oblivious to the tension sizzling between Tanner and me, or the pain meds were really kicking in, because he waved us away.

'Good. Then why don't you two go get acquainted and leave me to wallow in agony?'

'Your wish is my command, bro.' Tanner leaned down to give Remy a gentle hug, an unexpected gesture that made me like him a little when I didn't want to. 'I'll keep you posted. And don't worry, the patisserie will be fine.'

'Take care, Rem,' I said, skirting the bed to the opposite side of Tanner, before bending down to place a kiss on his cheek. 'Get well fast, okay?'

'I will.' Remy's cheeky grin alerted me to the fact I wouldn't like what he said next. 'You're in Tanner's capable hands now.'

Heat surged to my cheeks as I imagined exactly what it would feel like to be in those hands, literally.

Then I made the mistake of glancing up to see Tanner hold up the hands in question, the corners of his mouth curved in a devastating smile. 'Lucky you.'

Many words could be used to describe how I felt right at that very moment.

Lucky sure as hell wasn't one of them.

CHAPTER TWO

Tanner

I HADN'T BEEN kidding when I told Remy I was up for a challenge. But the cool blonde with glacial blue eyes and an attitude to match wasn't one of them.

A snowman could get frostbite next to that one.

From the first time she'd stared down her snooty nose at me, I had her pegged. Bored rich girl playing at baking goodies for a while. Probably like the ones she'd created in her state-of-the-art playroom kitchen as a kid, envisaging a prince charming with a mega bank account to come along and rescue her.

Yeah, women like her had the fairytale down pat.

Which begged the question: Why had she stuck around for a year?

Remy had given me the basics about his protégé during one of our phone calls about ten months ago. Said that one of his best customers had come into the patisserie one day, wild-eyed and dishevelled, begging for a job. It had been her dream to be a pastry chef apparently.

What a crock of shit.

I had no idea what game this Abby chick was playing, but the fact Remy had offered her the apartment over the patisserie while she got her life back together, and she was still there, meant I'd be keeping an eye on her and figuring out what her deal was.

Everybody had an angle. I'd learned that the hard way. So if the ice princess was taking advantage of my brother I'd kick her out on her sweet ass so fast she wouldn't see it coming. And it was sweet. Very, from what I'd glimpsed when she'd bent over to kiss Remy.

It had been a touching gesture, indicating a depth of affection that could be construed as genuine, if I didn't know better.

Women like her were masters at deception, and if her endgame was to fool my brother—maybe into giving her a piece of the action at Le Miel—she was in for a rude shock.

Remy had always been too kind-hearted; that was his problem. Probably one of the reasons Dad had tolerated him and despised me.

'We should head back to the patisserie,' Abby said as we exited the hospital. 'Makayla, one of the staff, will be run off her feet.'

'Not so fast, Sweet Thing.' My hand shot out, touching the small of her back, and a shock akin to electricity sizzled up my arm. 'We need to get acquainted first.'

She stared at me like I'd suggested we get naked to do it, and I grinned. The thought wasn't totally unpalatable, considering how much fun it would be to rattle that impenetrable façade.

'I meant let's grab a coffee at that café down by the water, but if you had something else in mind I'm up for it.' I threw in a wink, knowing it would rile her more than anything else I could say.

Predictably, she drew herself up to an impressive five-ten. Tall for a woman. I preferred them petite and pliable, not big and bristly.

'*Sweet thing* isn't my name,' she said, chin tilted, haughty as hell.

'Would you like it to be?' I leaned in, expecting her to jump back like a startled cat.

When she held her ground and glared at me with those big blue eyes, an unusual azure similar to a glacier I'd seen in New Zealand once, I had to admire her a little.

'Here's the deal. I love my job and I respect your brother. He gave me a chance when no one else would, and I'm not going to screw this up over some big-mouthed Romeo who can't keep it in his pants. Got it?'

She jabbed me in the chest with a finger. She actually *jabbed* me. And I admired her all the more for having the balls to stand up to my in-your-face innuendos to get a rise out of her.

'So quit the bullshit flirting and let's talk business.'

I couldn't resist one more. 'Dirty business?'

'Jeez, you're annoying,' she muttered under her breath as she stomped away.

Okay, so maybe I'd pushed too far but getting her so wound up had its advantages. Namely giving me an unimpeded view of her ass.

My earlier assessment had been correct. It was sweet. Taut and rounded, highlighted to perfection in the tight black pants worn by staff at the patisserie.

The patisserie...

I'd promised Remy to ensure it ran smoothly in his

absence, and I always kept my promises. I might be a prick who didn't let anyone get too close but Remy was different. He was my blood. And I owed him.

Which meant I needed to play nice with little miss sweet cheeks.

'Hey, wait up.' I caught up to her in a few strides. 'Look, you can blame my idiocy on jet lag, considering I only got in from LA late last night.'

She shot me an exasperated glance that indicated she hadn't thawed in the slightest.

'Let's have that coffee, and I promise to behave.' I held up my hands to show I had no tricks up my sleeves. 'What do you say?'

She hesitated, gnawing her bottom lip, and damned if the innocuous action didn't shoot straight to my cock. Contrary to popular belief, I didn't screw everything that walked and it had been a few months since I'd been with a woman.

Time to rectify that if the ice princess got me horny with a simple lip-nibble.

'Come on, Abby, I don't bite.' I refrained from adding, 'only if you ask nicely', because that wasn't helping the hard-on situation.

After what seemed like an eternity, she managed a terse nod. 'Fine.'

But it wasn't. Because as we strolled the last fifty metres to the café I caught a whiff of her fragrance on the wind. An intoxicating blend of vanilla and coconut, and I wondered if she tasted as good as she smelt.

Shit. Remy would castrate me if I screwed around with his protégé. Not that I wanted to. Taunting was one thing, following through another.

But as another gust of wind blew blond strands of

hair into her face and my fingers itched with the urge to brush them away, I knew working alongside Abby would be a long four weeks.

I'd craved a challenge.

Looked like I'd got one.

CHAPTER THREE

Abby

I DIDN'T HAVE time for this.

I should head back to Le Miel and make sure Makayla had everything under control.

Instead, I had to play nice with *him*.

'This table suit?' Tanner gestured to the only vacant table for two outside the café. A cosy table.

Swallowing my first retort of 'hell no', I nodded. 'Let's get this done so I can head back to the patisserie.'

'Why the hurry to get rid of me?' He pulled out my chair, a gentlemanly gesture at odds with the raw toughness that radiated off him. 'I told you I'd behave.'

I managed a tight smile in thanks as I sat, well aware that Tanner's version of 'behaving' and mine would be continents apart.

'What'll you have?' He sat and pushed his shirt-sleeves up, revealing heavily inked arms.

I didn't like tattoos. Couldn't fathom what drove a person to scar their skin like that. But as Tanner leaned his forearms on the table, I couldn't tear my gaze away from the sheer artistic beauty that started above his wrists and wound its way up.

Elaborate vines. Stunning roses. Intricate motifs. Symbols I couldn't decipher from this distance but wanted to get closer to.

I found myself inadvertently leaning forward before realising what I was doing, and when I glanced up Tanner grinned like he knew exactly how fascinating I found him.

'See anything you like?'

'No,' I snapped, sounding uptight and prudish, the situation made worse by the wash of heat flushing my cheeks.

'They extend a lot further than my arms,' he said, his voice low and gravelly, the underlying hint of naughtiness making my thighs clench. 'In case you were wondering.'

'I don't like tattoos,' I said, making a mockery of my supercilious declaration when my gaze strayed to those forearms again.

Strong. Sinuous. Sexy.

Damn.

'Many people don't.' He shrugged, like my opinion meant little. 'They see tats and think bikers and drug lords. They don't get the artistic angle at all.'

'You like art?'

It was the safe thing to say, a conversation starter that would get us off the topic of his tattoos and his body. I hoped.

'I like ink.' He leaned back in his chair and interlocked his hands behind his head, a guy comfortable in his own skin.

Which he revealed more of as the hem of his shirt

rode up and I got a tantalising glimpse of more ink on his lower belly. I couldn't make out the design, but it looked suspiciously like a cutlass and a hook.

'A pirate, seriously?' The words popped out before I could stop them and while I was horrified I'd articulated my thoughts, he laughed so loud nearby patrons turned to stare.

'Don't look so shocked,' he drawled, filling our glasses from the water bottle between us. 'I like a good pillage like the next pirate.'

I compressed my lips before I blurted anything else. Like how I'd rather walk the plank than be pillaged by him.

Though that wasn't entirely true, and after my disastrous marriage, I'd made a promise to myself to never lie again—especially to myself.

In less than thirty minutes, Tanner King had made me feel more alive than I had in years. He riled me. He taunted me. His cocky, laid-back attitude annoyed the crap out of me.

But I liked the buzz making my skin prickle and the weird hollow feeling deep in my belly. Like I was missing something. Like I craved something.

Much to my horror, I had to admit that he turned me on a little. A lot. Whatever.

Bastard.

'Let me guess. You're going to make some crude remark about what constitutes the pirate's peg leg.'

He laughed again, the crinkles at the corners of his eyes endearingly cute. 'You're funny. I like that in a woman.'

The natural retort, that he'd like all women, hovered on the tip of my tongue but a waitress appeared and after she'd taken our orders—double shot espresso for him, soy latte for me—I was back to being scrutinised by his intense golden gaze and liking it too much.

I needed to get this meeting back on solid ground. Professional. Far from charming smiles and pirate peg legs.

'Remy told me you've run restaurants?'

A shadow clouded his eyes for a moment, a hint of sadness, before he blinked and I wondered if I'd imagined it. 'Yeah, but nightclubs are more my thing.'

I bet. I could imagine him prowling around a dim room like a panther stalking its prey at night. Senses on high alert. Watching. Waiting. Before pouncing on some poor unsuspecting female.

Though with the amount of testosterone radiating off his taut body, maybe I should amend that to lucky female.

'I haven't seen you around the patisserie?'

He'd been toying with the cutlery on the table and he stilled, like I'd taken a shot at him for not being around for his brother. 'I've been working in London and LA. Helping friends set up similar nightclubs to the ones I run here.'

'How altruistic.' The sarcasm slipped out before I could stop it and I wasn't surprised when he frowned at me. 'Sorry, that sounded bitchy. It's an important day for me and then Remy fell and I was so worried… about him and the patisserie and getting everything done…'

Great, now I sounded like a rambling loser. But to Tanner's credit, he didn't make a joke. In fact, he looked surprisingly serious, the first time I'd seen him like this in our brief acquaintance. I liked it. That he could lose the clown act when called for.

'You won't have to do it on your own, that's why I'm here,' he said, eyeballing me with curiosity. 'As for my big brother, he'll be fine.'

He paused, a glimmer of a frown slashing his brows. 'So it's an important day, huh? What's the occasion? You getting hitched?'

I snorted and wrinkled my nose. 'Been there. Done that. Tore the bouquet to pieces.'

'You're married?'

'As of today, officially divorced.' I made jazz hands. 'Woop-de-freaking-do.'

'Being divorced has gotta be better than being married,' he said, making *married* sound like a dirty word.

'It is when you're married to a cold, heartless dweeb because it seemed the right thing to do at the time.'

Even now I could see that day so clearly. The rear garden of my parents' harbourside mansion converted into a winter wonderland. Massive marquees. White chiffon draping everything. Fairy lights twinkling in the perfectly manicured trees. Five hundred of their closest acquaintances. And Bardley, waiting at the altar, staring at me with avarice, like he'd scored a prized portfolio.

I should've made a run for it then. But I'd been a people-pleaser to the end, and given up my soul in the process.

Never, ever, again.

'I thought women viewed marriage as hearts and flowers and all that crap, not something to do because it's *right*.' He made cutesy inverted comma signs with his fingers. 'Want to talk about it?'

His mouth eased into a sexy smile. 'Tell Uncle Tanner all your dirty little secrets.'

If he only knew.

'No dirt and it's not a secret. Married at twenty-one to a guy I'd virtually grown up with. Family friends. Our folks pushed us together constantly so it seemed like a natural progression to get married.'

My chest tightened at the memory of what had happened after I'd said 'I do'. Of how Bardley had morphed into a sadistic, controlling monster. 'Moved into Vaucluse. Perfect house. Perfect life. Except it wasn't so perfect…'

I trailed off, wondering why the hell I was revealing all this to a virtual stranger. Then again, maybe that was the attraction. I didn't know Tanner and he knew jack about me. Today was a turning point for me. Proof that I'd walked away from my old life. I'd been counting down the days until I was officially divorced and who knew? Maybe once I'd purged all the crap I'd bottled up for so long I might be able to finally accept that the past didn't control me any more.

'Did the bastard hit you?' Tanner growled, and I glanced up, surprised to see his hands clenched into fists. 'I don't care if you're divorced. Tell me where to find the prick and I'll beat him to a pulp.'

'Whoa, he-man.' I held up my hands. 'Bardley was emotionally and verbally abusive, but he never laid a finger on me.'

'That other shit's just as bad,' he muttered, his

hands relaxing a little. 'What kind of a dickhead name is Bardley, anyway?'

I smiled, his ferociousness as sexy as the rest of him.

'"That other shit" is why I left him. It got to a point where I couldn't take it any more...' I shook my head, remembering the exact moment I'd taken control of my life.

He'd belittled me in front of his friends, forcing me to try water-skiing when he knew I was petrified of any water above bathtub level. I ended up spraining my wrist after taking a bad tumble the first time I tried to stand on the skis. It had been a suspected fracture. Bardley had mocked me. Been totally indifferent to my pain. Had called me names.

I'd packed with my one good hand that night and taken a cab to a motel. Spent a good hour emptying my bank accounts and maxing out my credit cards by paying a top lawyer most of his fee in advance.

I regretted being a fool. Being the kind of woman to put up with that treatment from anyone. Then again, I'd been doing it my entire life, so I guess my idiocy had been ingrained from birth.

'So what's the plan?'

'Plan?' I mimicked, coming back to the present, almost surprised to find myself sitting at a harbourside café on a glorious spring day with a seriously hot guy.

'To celebrate your divorce.' He lowered his voice. 'You have got something in mind to celebrate, right?'

'I'd envisaged leaving the patisserie early tonight to kick back with a spectacular red wine and Channing Tatum, but it looks like I'll be stuck working 'til late, taking over Remy's duties and prepping for tomorrow.'

He rolled his eyes, his upper lip curled in derision. 'What is it with women and Channing Tatum?'

'Hot bod. Chiselled jaw. And the guy has the moves. What's not to like?'

'He's a fantasy.' He sniggered, a decidedly wicked sound. 'Wouldn't you prefer a real man?'

I saw the challenge in Tanner's unwavering stare. Taunting me. Encouraging me to say yes.

I knew what he was offering.

A night of debauchery.

A night to wipe away sour memories of my marriage.

A night to come alive.

But I had to work with this guy for the next four weeks. Remy was depending on me, and no way in hell would I screw up his faith in me by screwing his brother.

'I'd prefer if we drank our coffees and got back to the patisserie,' I said, exhaling in relief when the waitress appeared to place our order on the table.

'Fair enough,' he said, but he wasn't done yet. The twinkle in his eyes alerted me to the fact that every second I had to spend with him over the next month would be pure, unadulterated torture. 'But if you want to ditch the fantasy in favour of the real thing, you know where to find me.'

He picked up his small coffee cup and raised it in my direction. 'Here's to a good working relationship, real-life celebrations and finding the elusive peg leg.'

I choked on my first sip of latte and he laughed, a low, sexy chuckle that sent a jolt of longing through me.

Yeah, it was going to be a *long* four weeks.

CHAPTER FOUR

Tanner

I TOOK ONE step into Le Miel and wished I'd said hell no when Remy asked me to help him out.

There was a reason I avoided the patisserie. With its polished honey floorboards, sunlight spilling inside and the tempting aromas of warm yeast and sugar heavy in the air, it reminded me of home.

Of Mum.

I'd been ten when she died, twenty long years ago. My memories of her might have faded with time but I'd never forget standing next to her in the kitchen while she baked. Passing her cups of flour. Gently handling eggs. Having my own board to roll pastry on. Licking icing from my sticky fingers.

Our kitchen had been huge, almost industrial-sized. Mum had run a makeshift cupcake business from home but mostly she'd loved to cook. It was her passion, like she'd been my father's, the Frenchwoman who'd stolen his heart on a gap-year trip to Paris.

Pity the romance hadn't lasted.

From what Remy told me, Dad had taken one look at Claudette Allard and she'd become the number one woman in his life. They'd married in two months, had Remy a year later and I'd arrived five years later. And from what I'd overheard that fateful day Mum had died, everything had turned to shit about then.

Dad avoided the kitchen and even as a youngster I'd been glad. We were happier when he wasn't around, me, Mum and Remy.

I'd loved those days when we'd all be in there together: Mum smacking my hand for sneaking a croissant before it had cooled. Remy helping me with a tricky letter on the icing. Me proudly presenting Mum with her favourite chocolate cupcake that I'd baked from scratch. Just the three of us, laughing and joking around. Happy. Together.

Until that day I'd heard my parents argue, the kind of argument that had imprinted on my brain no matter how many times, how many drinks and how many women I'd used to dislodge it. The day Mum had been so upset she'd rushed out of the house, got in her car and been killed in a crash, leaving us with Dad.

And my hell had begun.

'You okay?'

I glanced down to see Abby's hand lightly resting on my forearm, concern crinkling her brow.

Annoyed I'd let memories get to me, I shrugged off her touch. 'Yeah. Let's get started.'

She didn't believe me. She had this way of staring at me with those deep blue eyes like she could see right through me. It was disconcerting.

No one saw the real me. Ever.

'You've been here before, right?'

I nodded. 'Not for a while though.'

She didn't ask why but I could see her condemnation in the flattening of her lips.

'I'll show you Remy's office as that's where you'll be working.'

So she didn't know I could cook? Interesting. I could have a lot of fun showing Miss Prim and Proper exactly what I could do with a rolling pin.

'Lead the way,' I said, with a mock bow, biting back a laugh when she gritted her teeth.

This could be fun if I concentrated on baiting my cool co-worker rather than mentally rehashing maudlin memories.

The late-morning crowd had thinned to a few mums with toddlers and an older couple reading the newspaper. From the few times I'd been here over the years, I knew early mornings and lunchtimes were hectic. Remy would have hired staff accordingly but a sliver of worry niggled.

I ran successful nightclubs employing hundreds of people. I'd run restaurants up and down the eastern seaboard. So why the touch of anxiety that I could be in over my head with one patisserie?

Because this place was Remy's pride and joy, and I knew it. I owed my brother a lot. He'd cheered me up when I'd been young and reeling from Dad's subtle hatred, even if he'd been oblivious as to the reason behind my sulks. He'd shown me how to cook, how to play footy, how to be a man by using clever words rather than my fists when kids teased me at school for not having a mum. He'd raised me when the old man had the decency to curl up his toes when I was fifteen, never complaining at being saddled with a recalcitrant teen when most guys were partying at twenty.

Remy was my hero, always had been, and the only person I let get close. So I'd make damn sure that not only did the patisserie continue business as usual, but also that it flourished.

As we passed the gleaming stainless-steel counter, a young guy popped up from behind it, balancing a stack of trays. Abby smiled and the poor guy almost dropped the trays. I didn't blame him. I hadn't seen the ice princess smile much since we'd met but when she did...*kapow.* I felt it like a kick to the guts.

'Shaun, I'd like you to meet Tanner King, Remy's brother. He'll be the boss around here 'til Remy's back on his feet.'

I stuck out my hand. 'Good to meet you.'

'You too.' Shaun placed the trays on the counter and shook my hand. Firmly. Earning him brownie points. 'Abby texted me earlier to let me know he's going to be okay. That's good news.'

'Sure is.' The kid couldn't have been more than eighteen yet for some reason the thought of Abby texting him about anything stung. Pathetic. 'Have you been working here long?'

'Two months,' he said, shooting Abby a scared look, like he expected I'd fire him on the spot. 'I've enrolled at a college to do pastry work, and I need the hours here as part of an apprenticeship.'

'You're in the right place.' I tempered my tone so the kid wouldn't look so damn frightened. 'Remy's the best.'

'He sure is.' A woman sauntered out from the corridor linking the shop to the kitchen.

If Abby was ice, this one was fire.

Flaming red hair, deep blue eyes and the body of

a lithe goddess. She moved like a dancer, confidence and strength, like she knew her place in the world and wasn't afraid to flaunt it. A stunner. Yet I felt nothing but appreciation for her as a beautiful woman, whereas Abby turned me on with a tilt of her snooty nose.

Go figure.

'Hi, I'm Makayla Tarrant, waitress extraordinaire.' She held out her hand and I shook it, a little relieved when there was no zing. 'Hope you're ready to roll up your shirtsleeves and get to work. Remy doesn't appreciate slackers around here.'

Abby appeared outraged, shoulders drawn back and icy glare back in full force, and I laughed, liking the other woman already.

'You'll be pleased to know I intend to work as hard as the rest of you while I'm here.' I pushed up my sleeves for emphasis, liking when Abby's gaze drifted to my forearms.

She'd been mesmerised when I'd done it earlier at the café, like she'd never seen ink before. A blush had appeared on her cheeks as she'd studied me, and I'd had the craziest impulse to strip off and show her exactly how much ink covered my body and where.

'Good, then let's get started.' Abby cleared her throat, oddly brusque, and that blush was back.

Oh, yeah, showing her the rest of my tats could be fun.

'Nice meeting you both,' I said, with a wave at Makayla and Shaun.

Shaun shot me a nervous smile and Makayla nodded, her gaze assessing, like she couldn't figure me out.

Join the long line, honey.

Abby strode down the corridor that led to the kitchen, and I followed, the aroma of sugar and cinnamon and buttery goodness getting stronger with every step.

For a moment, I couldn't breathe.

Sadness clogged my throat. Potent. Disorienting.

When she opened a door marked 'Office' off the corridor, I'd never been more grateful.

I couldn't enter the kitchen right now, not when some strange nostalgia gripped me, making me yearn for a past I'd left behind a long time ago.

'Remy's very organised, so you'll find everything documented in spreadsheets. Supply order forms. Current stock. Online orders. The works…' She trailed off as I slammed the door, wishing I could do the same on the memories swamping me. 'Tell me what's wrong.'

'Nothing,' I growled, annoyed that she was so insightful. 'Continue the induction.'

'No.' She folded her arms, her superiority annoying me as much as the relentless memories of how much I missed Mum. 'For some reason, being here has you rattled, and I need to know why so we can fix it.'

'Babe, you may be many things, a shrink isn't one of them.' I stalked towards her, covering the short distance between us. 'I don't need to be *fixed*.'

'I—I didn't mean it like that.' She took a small step back as I invaded her personal space. 'I want this place to run smoothly while Remy's away and if there's a problem I want it sorted now before it affects business.'

I admired her dedication to my brother. Not many employees would give a rat's ass about their boss's business. But no way in hell would I stand here and be analysed by her ladyship.

'So that's what's all-important to you, is it? Business?'

A tiny dent appeared between her brows, as if she didn't understand the question, before she nodded. 'Of course. Remy gave me a chance when my life was down the toilet. I owe him. And I won't have you breezing in here on the pretext of helping and screwing it up.'

My respect ratcheted up further. I didn't like many people in this world let alone respect them, so I decided to wind her up a little to detract from the flood of uncharacteristic emotions swamping me the last few minutes.

'If you're all business, when do you have time for pleasure?'

Her lips parted in a surprised little O and I took it a step further.

'You do know what *pleasure* is?'

I leaned in, close enough to smell the sweetness of vanilla in her hair, close enough to see her porcelain skin was one hundred percent natural and unadorned by make-up, close enough to kiss her if I was so inclined.

'Back off,' she said, her fighting words at odds with the soft, breathy way she uttered them.

'Make me.' I squared my shoulders, wondering when I'd last enjoyed sparring with a woman this much.

'You're such a...child,' she muttered, and I laughed at how she must've watered down that insult.

'And you're all woman.' I leaned against a filing

cabinet, knowing she'd have to push past me to get out. 'But a prickly one. Don't you ever lighten up?'

Anger sparked in her eyes, flecks of vibrant emerald and sizzling sapphire among the blue. 'I haven't got time to lighten up. I work ten-hour days here, five days a week, while attending classes one day a week to complete my apprenticeship. On Sunday, my one day off, I do extensive research to update my blog so that people will know who the hell I am if I eventually save up enough to open my own place one day.'

Her chest heaved with indignation as she tried to shove past me. 'So why don't *you* lighten the hell up and give me a freaking break?'

I should've felt bad for pushing her to this point. I didn't. Because if her icy façade had turned me on, it had nothing on this outraged, furious woman.

She was spectacular.

So I calmed her down the only way I knew how.

I hauled her against me and kissed her.

I caught her off guard, her gasp of surprise all I needed to invade her mouth, my tongue taunting hers as much as my words.

I'd expected her to retreat. To possibly bite me. I didn't expect the low moan that emanated from the back of her throat, like a primitive growl that reverberated all the way down to my soul. Or the way she pushed against me, so hard my back slammed against the filing cabinet.

The ice princess liked it rough and ready. Who knew?

I ravaged her mouth, palming her breast and tweaking a nipple as she writhed against me. Hot. Wanton. Abandoned.

If she didn't stop, I wouldn't be able to and, as much as I'd like to, screwing her on Remy's desk my first day here wasn't part of the plan.

Remy.

With an anguished groan I wrenched my mouth from hers, stunned I'd let it get this far.

What was it about this woman that made me forget boundaries let alone my own name?

'I need to get to work.' I pushed past her like nothing had happened and took a seat behind the desk, adjusting myself as I did so and wishing my brother had the smarts to install a shower at his workplace.

I'd never needed a cold shower so frigging badly.

Abby stared at me in open-mouthed disbelief. I knew the feeling. I couldn't believe we'd just done that either.

'I—you—shit,' she muttered, shaking her head as I tried not to notice her reddened lips and her flushed cheeks, blond tendrils sticking out all over the place.

She looked like we'd done a lot more than kiss, and my cock throbbed again.

'Don't expect me to apologise for that,' I said, waving her away in a cruel dismissal, like the kiss meant nothing.

When in fact I needed her to leave ASAP so I wouldn't be tempted for a repeat. Next time, I might not be able to stop.

'I don't expect anything from you.' The haughtiness was back as she tilted her chin and stared down her nose at me. 'Not a single bloody thing.'

She slammed the door on her way out.

I didn't blame her.

CHAPTER FIVE

Abby

IF THERE WERE awards handed out to people for the art of pretending, I'd have an entire shelf full. A room full. An entire house full. I'd be in the academy's hall of freaking fame.

I'd done it my whole life. Pretending I liked the handcrafted silver jewellery box for my seventh birthday when I'd wanted a backyard cricket set. Pretending I liked having a fully catered disco party for my thirteenth birthday when I'd wanted to have fish and chips on the beach with my only friend. Pretending I didn't mind having a lavish society wedding when I would've been happy swapping vows at the register office.

Yeah, I was an expert at pretence. A goddamn queen. Which was how I managed to get through the rest of the day, creating brioche and baguettes and *pains au chocolat*, like that kiss had never happened.

That kiss.

Six hours later, it still haunted me.

Powerful and commanding and so damned passionate I got damp just thinking about it.

I'd never, ever, been kissed like that.

Like stepping into a raging inferno, consumed by heat from the inside out and not giving a damn.

I'd lost it. The moment his mouth covered mine I hadn't been able to think. Hadn't wanted to, if I was completely honest. Because kissing Tanner King put a full stop on my old life and kickstarted my new.

I'd wanted to celebrate with Channing tonight. Instead, I'd got a brief taste of Tanner and I wasn't disappointed. Angry at myself for letting it happen. Confused why he'd done it. And seriously peed off. But never disappointed.

God, the man could kiss.

If I was the queen of pretending, he was the master of manipulating lips.

My hand drifted upward to my mouth and a fingertip traced my bottom lip. I could swear it still tingled from the way he'd devoured me.

'All locked up, Abs.'

I jumped and spun around, hoping Makayla hadn't seen me. 'Thanks.'

She grinned and pointed to the small table set up in the kitchen where staff took their meal breaks. 'Why don't you sit and tell me all about the dishy Tanner while I fix us a hot chocolate?'

'Nothing to tell,' I said, far too quickly, and Makayla raised a knowing brow.

'You've been avoiding the office all afternoon and blushing at random times for no reason so I beg to differ, my friend.' Makayla tittered as she performed a little pirouette, something she did often, as if to keep her dance training at the forefront of her mind. 'Plus I just saw you staring into space and touching your lip, so I'm guessing you're fantasising about Hot Stuff kissing you.'

'You're too damn perceptive for your own good,' I muttered, but took a seat at the table anyway. 'Make mine a double.'

'Two giant marshmallows coming up,' she said, busying herself at the stove. 'Have to say, it's nice to see you lust over a guy. In the three months I've been here, you haven't mentioned anyone let alone been out on a date.'

Was I that pathetic? Considering I'd avoided men for the last twelve months since Bardley the Bastard, probably.

'Who said I'm lusting over Tanner?'

Makayla beamed as she poured hot chocolate into two mugs. 'Sweetie, it's all over your face.'

'Am I that easy to read?'

'I'm good at reading people.' Makayla plopped two marshmallows in each mug and headed for the table. 'Got a ton of experience at an old job.'

Sadness downturned her mouth for a moment, like it had been a less than pleasant experience, before her signature smile was back and she visibly brightened. Makayla spent all her spare time attending dance auditions and had worked in a few theatre productions. Maybe she needed to get a read on the competition?

'It's probably my self-imposed year-long drought—'

'You haven't been with a guy in a *year*?' Makayla squealed and mimicked a faint as I rolled my eyes.

'Yeah, I'm that much of a sad case.'

It wasn't until that moment I realised I was. Sad. My marriage might have been bland at best, but I missed the intimacy of having someone to debrief with at the end of a day. Of having a male perspective on life. Of being with a guy, even if the sex had been as lacklustre as the marriage.

Maybe that was why I'd enjoyed Tanner's kiss so much?

Yeah, and downplaying it would make me forget it in a hurry. Not.

'You need to get out more,' Makayla declared, her forehead crinkled in thought. 'A night out on the town. You and me. Drinks. Dancing. Deviously scoping out hot guys.'

'Nightclubs aren't really my thing—'

'Bull.' Makayla waggled her finger at me. 'I'm not taking no for an answer. If you're lusting over our new boss on the first day, you need to get laid.'

'I'm not a guy—'

'Girls have needs too, and after a year? Sweetie, you must be pretty damn needy.'

I laughed as Makayla wiggled her eyebrows.

'There's this fabulous club, the hottest dance venue in Sydney, called Embue. We're going. Tomorrow night.' She did another jig. 'So get your dancing shoes on, baby, because I'm not taking no for an answer.'

I'd seen Makayla like this before, when she'd railroaded me last month into buying an exquisite rose silk scarf I couldn't afford at The Rocks market. And before that, when she'd insisted I attend an art gallery opening that featured the weirdest nude paintings.

She wouldn't give up until I said yes, so I sighed. 'What kind of weird name is Embue?'

'It means *steamy* in French.' Makayla winked and fanned her face. 'Don't you want to get all steamed up over some guy?'

I already was and that was the problem. Because heading out to some dark, dingy nightclub to scope out men wouldn't make me forget Tanner and the potency of his kiss.

I'd need to meet Channing or his equivalent for that to happen and the odds were a billion to one of any guy remotely coming close to my screen idol.

But I had a feeling Makayla wouldn't let up. She'd asked me out to go clubbing several times since she'd started working here and we'd become friends, and I'd fobbed her off with excuses of homework.

With school holidays coming up and the universities winding down, she wouldn't buy that excuse this time.

I gave a resigned shrug. 'Okay. Let's do it.'

Makayla clapped her hands, excitement making her eyes glitter. 'Two babes out to shake things up. Can't wait.'

I could, but I needed something—maybe even someone—to distract me from this insane attraction to Tanner.

A night out could be just the thing I needed.

CHAPTER SIX

Tanner

I HAD TO hand it to my brother. He sure knew how to run a business. Le Miel turned a handy profit and had the potential to expand if the boutique next door ever accepted his generous offer to buy them out.

I'd studied the spreadsheets yesterday and today, and couldn't find a single weak spot.

Unlike me, who'd discovered a major one: for prim, snooty women who kissed like a frigging dream.

Even now, a day and a half later, I couldn't get that kiss out of my head. Which was plain crazy, considering the number of women I'd kissed over the years. I hadn't been in double figures for a long while so why did Abby, with those weird azure blue eyes and her cool façade, get to me so damn bad?

So I'd done what had to be done. Avoided her. Snuck out yesterday while she'd been in the kitchen with Makayla, and locked myself away in the office all day today.

We'd exchanged civil greetings this morning, that was it. Suited me fine. I didn't have time to be some society girl's plaything. Her walk on the wild side to celebrate her divorce.

Not that I wasn't interested. Sex with Abby had the potential to be phenomenal. Women coming out of a shitty marriage could go off like firecrackers.

But Remy would bust my balls if I inadvertently hurt her and she quit out of some misguided notion that any future chance meetings between us would be uncomfortable.

It had happened before, when I'd been young and dumb; had opened my first club and slept with my accountant. She'd been looking for more than a good time, despite her reassurances before things started up. When it soured she left and I'd lost the best damn accountant in the business.

No, I wouldn't be responsible for screwing this up for Remy, not when he'd spoken so highly of Abby when I'd called him last night and first thing this morning.

I'd keep my distance. Maybe even apologise for that kiss. Remy's business had steadily increased over the last year and, considering he recorded Abby's progress as part of her apprenticeship, looked like his protégé had been a big part of that.

Le Miel and Remy couldn't afford to lose Abby.

Which meant I had to keep the snake in its cage.

I glanced at the clock. After seven, when I needed to start my own work at nine. No time for a workout to ease the kinks out of my back. Sitting at a desk for twelve hours straight was for fools.

Pressing the tips of my fingers to my eyes, I did a few yoga breaths while rolling my shoulders. I heard the door open and when I opened my eyes, Abby stood in front of me, with a steaming espresso and an almond croissant.

'You've been working hard all day and haven't been out, so I thought you might like a snack?'

'You're an angel,' I said, meaning it, as the pungent Brazilian brew hit my nose and I inhaled greedily. 'Thanks.'

'You're welcome.'

A faint blush stained her cheeks, as if she wasn't used to praise, and damned if I wasn't catapulted straight back to yesterday morning when I'd kissed her.

Her blush had been deeper then, the blue of her eyes so damn crystal clear I could've drowned in them.

My cock hardened in agreement and I inwardly cursed. Remember Remy and Le Miel and a flourishing bottom line?

Down, boy.

She handed me the coffee and placed the plate on the desk. 'At the risk of sounding like a nag, you shouldn't lock yourself away in here all day and not eat.'

'Who said I don't have a secret stash of energy bars in the top drawer?'

She quirked an eyebrow. 'Do you?'

'Nah, but if it stops you nagging, I'll say it.'

She smiled and it softened her features from pretty to breathtaking. 'I'm heading out soon so are you okay to lock up?'

'Sure, go head.' I tapped my temple. 'The alarm combo is stashed away up here.'

The corners of her mouth twitched. 'Not sure how

you can remember any new numbers when you must have a phone book's worth stored up there already.'

I laughed, enjoying this softer side of her. 'Did you just make fun of my little black book?'

She held her thumb and forefinger an inch apart. 'A little.'

Surprised by her lighthearted sparring when I'd expected her to be gauche and standoffish after that kiss, I feigned indignation. 'I'll have you know my mental capacity is much less than you give me credit for, so I keep the thousands of women's phone numbers stored in my cell.'

'Little wonder you have such a big one—' Her lips clamped shut and her eyes widened in horror at her gaff.

'We are talking about my cell, right? Or are you still obsessing over my peg leg?'

The blush returned, deepening her cheeks to a rosy pink. 'It's been a long day. I really should go.'

'And I really should let you.'

But neither of us moved, our gazes locked in some invisible battle of wills while electricity sparked between us.

I had to do something to break this tenuous hold she had on me before I did something monumentally stupid, like kiss her again. And not stop at a kiss this time.

'I'm sorry for kissing you yesterday,' I blurted, not sorry at all. 'It was out of line. Blame it on my jet lag, concern over Remy and your unfailing knack of goading me.'

'Glad to know it wasn't my womanly charms,' she

said, her dry response tempered with a smile. 'Honestly? Don't worry about it. Forgotten, just like that.'

She snapped her fingers and damned if my ego didn't take a hit.

Forgotten? That made one of us.

'Anyway, got to go. Makayla's taking me clubbing.' She made it sound like her friend was dragging her for a root canal. 'See you tomorrow.'

'Yeah, see you.' I watched her walk out the door, my gaze riveted to her ass.

She worked those black pants like nothing else and I scowled, snatching up the croissant and jamming it into my mouth.

The buttery goodness melted on my tongue and I wondered if its creator would taste as good.

CHAPTER SEVEN

Abby

I'D ENVISAGED EMBUE being a one-room dive with mirrored walls, strobing lights and ear-splitting techno.

Thankfully, I was wrong.

'Isn't this place the coolest?' Makayla clung to my
arm and did a little jive on the spot. 'I've heard rave
reviews about it but this surpasses my expectations
by a mile.'

Mine too. Everything about the nightclub screamed
class, from the polished floorboards and soaring ceil-
ings to the chandelier hanging over the DJ's console,
placed smack-bang in the middle of the dance floor.

The dance floor circled the DJ like a giant shimmering oil slick, with golden velvet lounges in booths
surrounding it. Cream and gold were everywhere,
from the chiffon-covered walls to the coasters.

The entire effect was upscale elegance rather than
downtown disco.

I loved it.

As for the music, I actually recognised the song,
an upbeat nineties number that made me sway a little.

I elbowed Makayla. 'Should I make a confession now that I've never been to a nightclub?'

Makayla gripped my arm tighter and swung me around to face her. 'What the… I could've sworn you just said you'd never been to a nightclub?'

I held up my free hand. 'The truth and nothing but the truth.'

'What are you, a nun?' She released my arm, only to slug it. 'Girlfriend, either you've been in a cult or kidnapped by a madman who kept you locked up, because everyone on the planet has been to a nightclub at some point in their lives.'

Being part of the perfect Prendigasts had been like living in a cult, before being virtually kidnapped by Bardley and living in a prison of my own making.

'I got married at twenty-one.'

Makayla shook her head, a riot of glossy red curls tumbling over her bare shoulders dusted in glitter. 'But didn't you ever sneak into a nightclub underage? Go out with your friends from school?'

'I went to an all-girls private school and no, we didn't sneak out.'

We didn't do much of anything bar go on expensive shopping trips and have mani-pedis in the private comfort of our mansions. Not that I could call any of the girls I'd hung out with as friends. They'd been the bitchiest group I'd ever encountered, clones of their mothers whose only ambition was to find a rich, upper-class guy and marry him.

All they'd ever talked about was who had the latest designer bag, who had the most expensive car sitting in the garage for when they turned eighteen and which guys from the elite boys' schools were the best to shag.

How I'd longed to be part of those groups of girls who hung around together at the local shops, swapping frozen yoghurts and gossip while they waited for the school bus instead of Daddy's chauffeur.

Those girls had looked genuinely happy, despite their ripped blazers and holey jumpers. My folks had taught me from a young age that money could buy anything. They'd been wrong. I couldn't buy happiness, the kind I'd seen on those girls' faces.

'Sweetie, you need to start living.' Makayla gave me a gentle nudge towards the dance floor. 'Starting now.'

I wanted to let loose but I caught sight of myself in a floor-to-ceiling-length mirror and baulked.

Whereas Makayla fit in here with her dramatic make-up, sexily mussed hair, towering stilettos and a strapless figure-hugging purple mini, I looked like a grandma with my blow-dried hair, clear lip gloss and mascara, moderate heels and a staple sleeveless LBD that ended at my knees.

Who knew little black dresses had gone out of fashion around the same time I'd gone out of circulation?

'You're dancing. Now.' Makayla shoved me again and this time I let myself be propelled onto the dance floor, joining the throngs of writhing bodies moving in time to an old pop song about spinning around.

I liked music and always had the latest stuff on a playlist while I baked. But bopping around a kitchen and moving my body in front of a bunch of strangers were worlds apart.

Thankfully, nobody gave a flying fig as I started to shuffle my feet. Allowed my shoulders to relax and my hips to sway to the music.

'There you go. You're dancing and the ceiling hasn't caved in.' Makayla put her hand over her mouth in mock horror. 'Wow, you may even start having fun.'

'Bite me,' I yelled above the music, moving my body faster and adding a shimmy for good measure.

Makayla laughed and flung her arms in the air, her body sensual and sinuous as she executed moves I could never dream of pulling off.

After the first song, I lost track of how many we danced to. Daggy songs from the eighties mingled with the latest techno beats as I danced my ass off. Wiggling my hips. Shimmying my shoulders. Not caring that I jiggled in places I hadn't jiggled in a long time.

I enjoyed it. Until an old boyfriend of Makayla's slunk up to us and I quickly realised that three was a crowd.

I tapped her on the arm and gestured towards the bar. 'I'll leave you two alone.'

'You don't have to go.' Makayla's gaze swung between the guy and me and I could tell she was torn.

'Seriously, I'm zonked anyway. I'll just have a drink, then take a taxi home.'

'You sure?'

I nodded. 'Absolutely.' I leaned in and pecked her on the cheek. 'Go have fun.'

Still Makayla wavered. 'But tonight was supposed to be about you and finding some hot guy to end your drought.'

'Another time,' I said, giving her a gentle nudge in the direction of the guy waiting patiently for us to finish our conversation. 'Go. Be naughty enough for the both of us.'

A wicked gleam lit her eyes. 'I think I can manage that.'

I laughed and headed off the dance floor. I'd barely made it onto the polished boards before the guy had swept Makayla into his arms and they were doing some weird ritualistic dance that almost looked obscene.

Makayla was a lovely girl, I liked her a lot, and for one fleeting moment I wished I had half the *va-va-voom* factor she did.

With a sigh, I turned.

And ran smack-bang into Tanner.

CHAPTER EIGHT

Tanner

DOING THE ROUNDS of my clubs after putting in two long days at the patisserie wasn't my idea of fun, but I'd been away for almost a year and I wanted to do a stealth visit to see how the managers and staff were coping.

I needn't have worried. I only hired the best and the four clubs I'd visited so far were operating with precision. Embue was the last on my list and, like the rest, the managers were on top of things and the place was packed.

I'd planned on spending thirty minutes mingling, chatting with staff, getting a general feel where I could liven things up.

That plan shot to shit when I spied Abby. Writhing on the dance floor, arms flung wide, hips swaying, out of time with the music but dancing to some imaginary rhythm in her head.

Damned if it wasn't the most erotic thing I'd ever seen.

So I watched. My cock throbbing in time with some crap techno beat. Wanting her.

I saw some guy sleaze up to Makayla and they started chatting like long-lost lovers, all over each other. Leaving Abby a third wheel and about to leave.

She strode off the dance floor and twenty guys in the vicinity swivelled their heads to watch.

Not that she wore anything revealing. In fact, her modest black dress was practically outlandish in a sea of scantily clad women. But it was the way she carried herself. The set of her shoulders. The tilt of her head. The way her hips moved.

She exuded class. And every horndog in the place wanted to see if they could get behind that cool exterior and see how far she could be pushed to get off.

When one guy put down his drink and walked towards her, I made a move, cutting him off. 'Sorry, buddy, she's mine.'

A possessive statement I had no right making but no way in hell would I stand by and watch Abby have to fend off a bunch of horny pricks.

I reached out to tap her on the shoulder when she spun around and smacked into me.

'Whoa.' My arms shot out to grab her, her look of abject horror at finding me here making me want to tease the hell out of her. 'You've got to stop throwing yourself at me like this.'

She recovered her wits and her balance but I didn't release her. I liked having her this close, her nipples grazing my chest, her palpable heat warming my body, the sweat-slicked sheen to her skin.

She looked radiant.

'What are you doing here?'

'I own the place.' I shrugged, like it meant little, when in fact every club I owned was testament to how

far I'd come—and how far I'd proved Dad wrong.
'Haven't been here in a year so after I locked up at the
patisserie, I've done the rounds of my clubs, check-
ing up on things.'

To my surprise, she hadn't moved. In fact, now that
she'd recovered from the shock, she seemed perfectly
relaxed having me hold her arms like I wouldn't let go.

'The diligent boss, huh?'

'Something like that.'

We ran out of conversation, our gazes locked in
some kind of invisible heated battle, as I wondered
what it was about this woman that rattled my cage.

I wanted her with a fierceness I hadn't felt for a
long time. If ever. I dated. I screwed. I didn't do commitment. It worked well for me. Sex as exercise. Sex
for fun. Sex with women who knew the score and
didn't have any expectations.

Women nothing like Abby.

Abby would be a hearts and flowers kind of girl.
She'd told me about her bastard ex and the emotional
abuse, but who knew what kind of expectations she'd
put on the guy? Maybe he hadn't lived up to her high
standards? Maybe he'd lashed out verbally when he
couldn't handle it?

The moment I thought it, I felt guilty. Just because
I wanted Abby and knew that having her would be a
screw-up of monstrous proportions, I was trying to
find excuses and maligning her in the process. Not
cool.

'I should go.' She tried to back away, and the smart
thing to do would be to release her.

I tightened my hold. 'Would you like a tour? You

can have a drink and relax in the VIP room, then I'll get you a taxi.'

A refusal hovered on her lips. I saw them tremble with it before she clamped them tight and nodded.

Mentally calling myself everything from putz to dickhead, with a long list of obscenities in between, I led her to a shimmering gold curtain in the back corner and pulled it aside.

'After you.'

She hesitated, as if unsure of my intentions. Smart girl.

'What's wrong?'

She glanced sideways at me and, rather than see trepidation in her eyes, I glimpsed excitement. 'I've danced for about two hours nonstop and I'm about to faint if I don't get a drink. Could we skip the long tour and head straight to the bar?'

I smiled, her honesty refreshing. 'Sure, this way.'

We passed through the VIP room, filled with the usual crowd of elite sportsmen, WAGs, models and a visiting rap star from the US. Abby ogled a little but I had a feeling it was more about the way the women were draped all over the men than in any recognition for the VIPs.

For a woman in her early twenties, she was strangely naïve. Like she hadn't really lived. Rich girls like her would've gone to the best private school and been privy to parties from a young age. Sure, she might have married young but she'd been single for a year. She must've let loose over the last twelve months. So why the air of innocence that hovered over her like a cloud?

'Through here.' I slid a card over a digital lock and waited for the beep before pushing the door open.

Though no one used this room but me and I hadn't been in here for a year, I knew it would be immaculate and well stocked. My staff were nothing but professionals and word would've travelled fast from the other clubs that I'd probably drop by tonight.

'What would you like to drink?'

The door slid soundlessly shut behind us and I saw her glance at it, hesitate, before squaring her shoulders like she'd come to a decision.

She probably didn't trust me. I understood. But she had nothing to fear. I wouldn't mess with the status quo, no matter how much I wanted to ruffle that cool façade. Remy was too important to me, and I'd already screwed up enough in my lifetime to add yet another thing to feel guilty for.

'Sparkling water if you've got it, please.'

'For you, babe, anything.' I flashed her a quick grin, surprised when she smiled back. Maybe all that dancing had loosened up her reservations? 'Take a seat.'

But she didn't. Instead, she strolled around the room, inspecting it. 'What is this place?'

'My hideout.' I grabbed a bottle of mineral water out of the bar fridge, unscrewed the cap and poured it into a long glass, adding a sliver of lemon. 'When hosting a bunch of selfish, spoiled brats in the VIP room, I need a place to escape, and this is it.'

'It's nice,' she said, trailing her hand over the butter-soft black leather sofas, the small glass-topped desk in the corner, the display cabinet where I kept my awards. 'These all yours?'

'No, I mug every sportsman who comes in here and stash the loot in here,' I deadpanned, handing her the drink.

'Thanks.' She took the glass and downed the mineral water in several gulps as I stared at the almost convulsive movement of her throat and desperately tried not to imagine her doing something similar to me.

When she finished, she handed me the glass with a sheepish smile. 'I was parched.'

'Want a top-up?'

'Please.' She turned back to the awards as I poured her another glass. 'You've won a lot of stuff in the hospitality industry.'

'Awards are ego-strokers.' I handed her the glass, forcing myself to look away this time. I couldn't be any harder if I tried, grateful that I'd installed a bathroom in here too so the minute I put her in a cab I could take a cold shower. 'I prefer to see results in profit margins.'

She stilled, sadness creeping across her face. 'My father used to say that a lot. Always about the profit margins.'

'That's what matters most to savvy businessmen. That and a healthy portfolio.'

She screwed up her nose and damned if it wasn't the cutest thing I'd ever seen. 'Is that what you're all about? Because those tattoos speak more about rebelling against convention than caring about portfolios.'

'What's with you and my tats?' I shrugged out of my jacket, flung it on a sofa and rolled up my sleeves. 'Here. Look your fill. Then judge me some more.'

I had no idea where my outburst came from but I

felt like a jackass the moment she blushed in morti-
fication.

'I didn't mean to judge—I mean, I just haven't seen
tattoos up close and—'

'And you still haven't,' I muttered, hating that she'd
touched a sore spot without knowing it and I'd reacted
accordingly.

My tats were more than art.

They defined me.

At a time in my life when I hadn't been comfortable in my own skin, I took on a new one.

And having a woman like Abby judge me as just
another deadhead rebel because of my tats really
pissed me off.

'This would be looking at them up close,' I growled,
trying to tamp down my anger and failing as I unbut-
toned my shirt and shrugged it off. 'Here. Take a good
look. See if you can figure me out.'

I stood in front of her, hands on hips, defiant and
oddly vulnerable. I shouldn't care what she thought of
me. After Remy was back on his feet, I'd be outta here
and back on the road, heading to Bangkok or Ibiza or
Munich, creating successful clubs that would define
me more than my tats.

But I did care. And that was what pissed me off
the most.

I shouldn't give a flying fuck what Abby thought
of me.

Yet I did.

'I'm sorry,' she said, her apology soft and uncer-
tain, her gaze riveted to my chest. 'I've offended you.'

My anger dimmed a little as she scanned my chest
as if studying for an art exam. Her hungry gaze

gobbling me up and coming back for seconds. She couldn't look away.

I'd never been studied so closely, her scrutiny disconcerting. It felt like she could see through the tats to the real me beneath, the scared little boy I'd once been, desperate for approval.

'You're beautiful,' she said, taking a step closer to study me, gnawing on her bottom lip a little, the innocuous action making me want to throw her down on the sofa and take her.

Not 'the tats are beautiful', but '*you're* beautiful', her simple statement deflating what was left of my resentment.

Had it been a slip of the tongue or had she meant it? Because no one saw past my tats and a few moments ago she'd been like the rest, judging me for them.

'May I?' Before I could react she touched me, the briefest brush of her fingertips skating across my skin, tracing every inch of ink.

The Buddha. The peace sign outlined in flowers. The phoenix.

Symbols of my past.

My search for clarity.

My quest for harmony.

Rising out of the ashes of my childhood.

I held my breath as she moved lower, skirting around the pirate. Her fingertips light as air but making my skin burn.

'Seen enough?' I said through gritted teeth, regretting I'd let my anger get the better of me and done this.

Because daring her to look and expecting her to blush and turn away was far different from having Abby touch me like she wanted to explore my tats.

All over.

Her gaze lifted to mine and the blatant lust darkening her eyes to indigo blew me away.

Fuck, I was in trouble. So much trouble.

'Not nearly enough,' she murmured before placing her hand flush against my straining cock. 'All these pretty tattoos are an insult to your manhood, so you better show me that pirate's peg leg so my faith in you is restored.'

Laughter burst from deep within me as I held onto the last of my self-control.

'Abby, this is a bad idea. You're Remy's protégé and when this all turns to shit—'

'It won't,' she said, stroking me lightly through my jeans, shredding the last of my resolve. 'One night. That's all I'm asking for.'

She removed her hand and I inwardly cursed my misplaced chivalry. 'Though in fairness, I should disclose I haven't had sex in over a year so I may break you.'

I could resist the snooty princess.

I couldn't resist this playful, honest woman who stared at me like she could devour me in one gulp and come back for seconds.

'Fuck, Abby, you're making this hard—'

'I sure as hell hope so.' She cupped me again, firmer this time, and I lost it.

I dragged her forward and crushed her to me, grinding against her so she was in little doubt to exactly how this would go.

Hot, sweaty animalistic sex. Fast and furious and so fucking good.

She reacted like I'd set her alight. Slamming her

mouth to mine. Pushing me against the nearest wall. Climbing all over me.

It was the hottest frigging thing ever, having someone like her want someone like me so damn much.

Her tongue stroked mine, shy and darting one second, bold and commanding the next, as her hand sneaked between us to touch me.

She kissed aggressively, long, deep sweeps of her tongue totally at odds with the aloof front she usually presented. It turned me on even more, the contrast between fire and ice. Hot and cold. So frigging hot.

She'd go off when I entered her, I just knew it, and my cock ached with wanting to be inside her.

I palmed her breast, rolling the nipple between my thumb and forefinger, drawing a deep groan from her. Sensitive breasts, I liked that. I needed to feast on them, to suck on those nipples until she screamed.

But my mind momentarily blanked as she slid her hand inside my jocks. Wrapped her fingers around my cock. And squeezed.

'I want to see you,' she murmured against my mouth, nipping at my bottom lip while continuing to squeeze me. Stroke me. Undo me.

'Right back at you.' I hissed out a breath as her thumb rolled over the head of my cock, and I stilled her hand, withdrew it before I embarrassed myself.

There was something incredibly hot about a shy, reserved woman taking charge, and having her go for my package served to ratchet up the desire pounding through me to a relentless beat.

'Turn around.'

If my guttural growl frightened her, she didn't show it. Instead, her tongue darted out to moisten her bottom lip before she pouted. 'But I want to see the pirate. *All* of him.'

'You will, babe, trust me.' I flashed a wolfish grin. 'But first, I need to see all of you.'

Uncertainty flickered in her eyes, so I hit the dimmer switch, willing to do anything to make her more comfortable.

Anything but stop.

Because I'd ditched my reservations around the time she'd ditched hers and stuck her hand in my pants.

I couldn't stop this. I didn't want to.

Not when she'd articulated exactly what this was. A rebound fuck. We both knew the score and that made it okay.

She didn't expect hearts and flowers.

She wanted hard and fast.

After over a year of celibacy—I didn't have a frigging clue how that had happened considering how damn gorgeous she was—she wanted to use me to break the drought.

The good girl wanting the bad boy to make it all better, even if it was only for one night.

This I could do.

The moment she'd taken emotion out of the equation and shown me exactly what she wanted, I couldn't say no.

I understood wanting to obliterate the past with something a tad wild, something not entirely good, something to make you forget. Boy, did I understand.

'I want you,' she said, the vulnerability of a moment ago fading as she eyeballed me with unabashed hunger. 'Real bad.'

'The feeling's mutual, sweetheart.' I spun her around and homed in on her zipper. Slid the tab down, the rasp of metal against metal meshing with her soft pants of anticipation.

I imagined expanses of soft, creamy skin. Unblemished. Untarnished. The opposite of mine. When I hit the bottom she whimpered a little. I slid my hands up her back. Pushed the dress off her shoulders.

It pooled at her feet, leaving her in matching black satin bra and panties. French cut. Almost prophetic. I liked everything French. French food. French fries. French kissing. And French panties I could tear off with my teeth to feast on her.

Her skin was as beautiful as I'd imagined and I trailed my fingertips across the top of her ass, skirted her waist, drifted upward, loving how soft she felt. She trembled a little as I unhooked the bra and stepped closer to slide it off her arms.

'Beautiful,' I murmured in her ear as I slid my arms around her from behind to cup her breasts. To savour the weight of them. To flick her light brown nipples with my thumbs. 'I can't wait to taste you.'

She made an incoherent sound as her head lolled back a little and I captured her mouth, plucking at her nipples. A deep tongue-tangling kiss, assertive and greedy, as I marvelled at the sweet taste of her, the hot moistness of her mouth, a prelude to how she'd be when I feasted lower.

'More,' she demanded between kisses, and I was only too happy to oblige.

Without taking my mouth off hers, I spun her towards me and ground my hand against her mound.

She moaned and I pushed her panties down, waiting until she'd kicked them off before sliding my fingers between her slick folds, savouring how wet she was. For me.

'Tanner, please...'

I wanted to prolong this, to go down on her once, maybe twice, before finally getting off. But my own months of celibacy ensured I'd take things slow later.

We had all night.

I zeroed in on her clit. Circled it twice. Stunned when she came apart so damn fast.

I hadn't pegged her for a screamer but she made enough noise to make me thankful for the club's soundproofing in every room.

'Wow,' she said, her head sagging against my shoulder, her body trembling with aftershocks. 'I think I needed that.'

I chuckled, her bluntness refreshing. Women didn't articulate much after sex beyond asking where the shower was and implying they wanted another date.

'Plenty more where that came from,' I said, gently easing her away, unable to stop grinning like an idiot when I took in her tousled hair, flushed cheeks and swollen lips. 'In case you were wondering, I love giving head and I plan on going down on you several times tonight.'

Her mouth parted in a shocked O before I continued. 'But first, I need to fuck you. Think you can handle that?'

Her eyes glittered with desire as she nodded and reached for me.

I'd wanted to shuck my jeans and jocks off in record time, get protected and bury myself to the hilt inside her before I exploded. But I let her call the shots because this was her night.

She unsnapped the button on my jeans and, with unsteady hands, yanked the zipper down.

'Easy, babe. Inflicting a mortal injury on me at this stage won't do either of us any good.'

'I want to see you,' she said, eyes wide as she pushed my jeans down my legs, her hungry gaze riveted to the bulge in my jocks.

'Be my guest.' I toed off my shoes and socks, and kicked my jeans away. 'Though haven't you heard staring too long at a guy's cock makes you go blind?'

'I thought playing with it did that?'

I chuckled. Not so innocent after all. 'You're something else.'

A hint of sadness crept into her eyes and I cursed for inadvertently saying the wrong thing. 'You okay?'

Her teeth worried her bottom lip as she shook her head a little. 'I—I haven't done this a lot. And I'm not very good…'

'That useless prick.' An explosive rage filled me at the thought of what her ex had done to her self-esteem. 'Sweetheart, look at me.'

I placed my finger under her chin and tilted it up, the uncertainty clouding her eyes slugging me in the chest. 'It wouldn't matter to me if you were a frigging virgin. This thing between us is pretty damn hot. Fireworks hot. So when we get to the good stuff you'll forget that bastard who did a number on you because I guarantee any problems you had were with him, not you.'

'How can you be so sure—?'

I kissed her. I wouldn't give her any more time to doubt. I had to show her.

She ignited again, her hands everywhere. Grabbing my biceps. My waist. Moaning into my mouth as she dug her fingers into my ass like she couldn't get enough.

I lowered her onto the sofa and broke the kiss, hovering over her like some goddamn avenging angel as she stared at me in wide-eyed wonder.

'That thing you said earlier? About wanting to do me?' She didn't break eye contact as she shimmied out of her panties. 'Please do it.'

I bit back a smile at her avoiding the F word, considering she was naked in front of me, and I didn't have to be asked twice as my gaze zeroed in on nirvana. I liked a full bush and appreciated that she hadn't gone for the Brazilian job many women favoured these days.

'Now it's your turn,' she said, splayed on the sofa like a wanton sex goddess. 'I want to see all of you.'

I slipped my thumbs under the elastic of my jocks and pushed them down and she gasped as my cock sprang free.

'You're huge!' She blushed as she continued to stare, unable to look away. 'I mean, I haven't seen many before. In fact, only one, and that was less than impressive, but you're quite big…' She wolf-whistled and I laughed to hide my surprise that she'd only been with her ex.

No wonder she had reservations when it came to sex. If the guy had been clueless in the bedroom he would've shoved his insecurities onto her. Dickhead.

'And why does the pirate only have a torso?' An

impish smile curved her luscious lips. 'Would've been so much more fun to make *that* his peg leg.'

She pointed to my cock and I chuckled again. 'You're a very bad girl.'

'Not yet, but I'm hoping to be.' She crooked her finger at me. 'Come here and corrupt me.'

I knew this was her fantasy. To have me, the tattooed bad boy, fuck her to eradicate her boring past. Yet for one crazy, inane moment, I wanted her to see me as more than that.

I wanted her to see past my well-honed tough guy persona and want me, Tanner King. Really want *me*.

Annoyed, I grabbed my jeans off the floor and snagged a condom out of my wallet.

Her tongue darted out to moisten her lips as she watched me roll it on, her expression wondrous.

'You sure you're not a virgin?'

A faint pink stained her cheeks. 'I just haven't done it in this much light before.'

Shit. Her ex really must've been a dickhead not to want to see every inch of this glorious woman as he slid inside her.

With an exaggerated wink, I knelt next to the sofa. 'All the better to see you with, my dear.'

Her lips curved into a naughty smile. 'I want to watch too.'

Which meant I needed to put on a show she'd never forget.

But all my intentions to take things slow shot to shit when she slid her ankles apart and her thighs fell open. Giving me an eyeful of moist folds and exactly where I wanted to be.

I grabbed her legs and half turned her, so she was

slumped against the sofa with her legs dangling down. Dragging her towards me, I scooted forward on my knees, positioning myself while trying to stop the urge to drive into her and not stop until she screamed my name.

'It's even bigger close up,' she whispered, her audible awe making me grin.

'Maybe you're looking at it through a side mirror?'

She laughed and damned if it wasn't the sweetest sound I'd ever heard.

I didn't usually swap banter during sex. And I rarely laughed. I got in and out. Got the job done. Got off. Felt good. That was it.

And even though we hadn't got to the good part yet, sex with Abby was different.

We connected beyond the bits fitting together.

It disarmed me.

So I focussed on doing what I did best. Ensuring she had a good time.

'Watch me,' I commanded as I gripped my cock in my hand and pressed the head against her clit. Circling it. Rubbing into her slick folds and back again. Over and over until her breath came in pants and her hips shifted restlessly.

'That feels so good.' She propped up on her elbows to watch and I increased the pressure, gritting my teeth against the tension building in my balls.

I'd already warned her about taking this slower later and it would have to do because right now I needed to be inside her so damn bad.

'More,' she gritted out, sweat beading between her breasts as she started to writhe.

'You got it, sweetheart.'

I gave her clit one last rub and as her orgasm started I slid into her. Hard. To the hilt. Sheathed in tight, wet pussy.

Heaven.

I thrust into her fast, using my thumb on her clit as she screamed, desperate to milk every last drop of pleasure out of her.

She surged upward, bringing her breasts into my face, and I took one in my mouth, laving her tight nipple while thrusting into her.

'Too sensitive,' she gasped, wrenching her nipple from my mouth and leaning back on her outreached arms. 'Want. To. See.'

So I let her.

I slid in and out. Harder. Faster. Oblivious to everything but watching her, watching me.

Damned if it wasn't the hottest frigging thing I'd ever seen.

My balls tightened and my mind blanked the moment before I thrust into her one last time. As far as I could go.

The most intense pleasure crashed over me. Wiping me out. Mindless. Boneless.

Conscious of nothing but this woman.

Abby.

My eyes must've closed at some point because when I opened them Abby was staring at me like I'd just given her the keys to the best patisserie in Paris.

'That was amazing,' she whispered, reaching for me. 'I never knew it could be so good.'

'Just good?' I slid my arms around her, cradling her close. Another first for me after sex. I wasn't a cuddler. 'Guess I better lift my game for the rest of the night.'

I couldn't see her face with it buried against my chest, but I sensed her smile.

But as she continued to hang onto me like she'd never let go, the first feelings of remorse flooded me.

For me, this would be a night of amazing sex and I'd walk away in the morning. Back to being Tanner King, the guy everybody labelled, the guy everybody judged, the guy everybody tried to get close to but couldn't.

No matter how stupendously good the sex, tonight wouldn't change me.

Could Abby say the same?

CHAPTER NINE

Abby

I HURT. In places I've never hurt before.

Even now, fifteen hours since I left Tanner's bed in the wee small hours, my muscles twang as a reminder of what I've done.

And how much I enjoyed it.

I didn't know whether to be relieved or annoyed when Tanner didn't front at Le Miel today. Whatever his reason, I couldn't keep the smile off my face.

What we'd done at the club, and later at his apartment…defied logic.

I should never have had sex with Tanner.

So why did I not give a damn that I had?

When he'd taken me to that private room at his club, I'd anticipated having a drink, then leaving. Then he'd got angry, taken off his shirt and I'd lost it.

I didn't usually ogle guys. Sure, I appreciated a fine male body on Bondi Beach in summer like any woman with eyes in her head, but I didn't fantasise about what guys looked like underneath their clothes.

Yet the second Tanner had shrugged off his shirt

in defiance I'd wanted to see more. I'd wanted to see all of him.

I must've said the wrong thing and his misplaced anger had prompted him to strip. That was the point I should've called for a cab. Or laughed it off as a joke. Or done anything other than practically drool all over him.

He'd been a good sport about my naivety. Had tried to put me at ease with banter and I'd appreciated it. What I didn't appreciate was my own stupidity wishing I could have more of him.

When I quashed my voice of reason and my inner vixen insisted I deserved one night of sexy fun, it should've ended there. One night.

But after he'd pleasured me countless times with his mouth, his fingers and his very talented and sizeable appendage, I wanted more.

Of course, I hadn't said anything. Instead, I'd been the epitome of casual, like I had one-night stands every day of the week, when he'd kissed me goodnight. If he'd seen through my bravado act, he didn't call me on it. For that, I was grateful.

Because I'd bolted in the wee small hours when he'd been asleep, and during the twenty-minute ride from his penthouse apartment in the city to my apartment over Le Miel I replayed every single moment of our night together and knew that acting like last night didn't mean anything the next time I saw Tanner would take monumental acting skills I didn't possess.

Bardley had always taunted me for being too readable. But he'd been wrong. If I were that easy to read he would've seen my loathing for him on my face every single day.

Thanks to Tanner, I now knew our lacklustre sex life hadn't been my fault. How many times had Bardley called me frigid or cold or worse? Saying I didn't turn him on. That I was as useless in the bedroom as I was in the kitchen.

I hadn't cared about the sex, but insulting my cooking had been a low blow, particularly since I knew I baked like a dream even back then.

Screw him.

Though thankfully, I'd never have to do that again and courtesy of last night I'd replaced memories of a sad sex life with phenomenally amazing erotic ones.

'You're daydreaming again.' Makayla bumped me with her hip. 'You sure you didn't pick up at Embue?'

I felt heat flush my cheeks but I feigned nonchalance as I scrubbed my station. We'd been busy today, frantic, supplying a local private school with pastries for a teacher conference, so I'd managed to avoid Makayla's interrogation. Until now.

'I'm not the one with a story to tell,' I said, pasting a bright smile on my face. 'You and what's-his-name looked mighty cosy when I left last night.'

Makayla screwed up her face. 'There's a reason you date a guy and don't go back.' She held up her little finger and let it droop. 'I'm smarter than that.'

I laughed, wondering what Makayla would say if she knew that a pinkie wouldn't come close to describing Tanner.

'What about you?' Makayla grinned as she dried her hands on a dishcloth. 'You're not still mooning over our dishy boss?'

If only she knew the half of it.

'Don't be silly.'

'Pity he's working off-site today. He brightens up the scenery.' Makayla pursed her lips and tapped them. 'He's nothing like Remy, is he?'

She got that right. Remy and Tanner might be biological brothers but that was where the similarities ended. I couldn't think of two siblings who were so different.

'Yeah, they're nothing alike,' I said, grateful Makayla had moved off the topic of last night and onto safer ground.

'I'm not just talking about looks.' Makayla struck a strong-man pose. 'Tanner's like this big tough guy who swaggers around, and Remy's soft and gentle.'

Tanner could be soft and gentle when it counted, and I'd counted last night. Many times.

'Do you know much about their background?' Makayla leaned against the bench. 'I don't know Remy that well but you've worked here for a year. What's the story?'

I shrugged. 'We don't talk much about our pasts.'

That was the truth. I'd divulged the basics to Remy about my crappy marriage and my dreams to become a pastry chef. He'd told me he'd opened this place many years ago, had never met the right woman and his only living family was Tanner.

When we chatted during a rare lull in our busy days, we talked pastries, the latest cooking reality show on TV and gave our critiques of the newest cookbooks.

I valued our friendship, especially since he'd offered me a place to live and a job when I'd needed it most, but we weren't the kind of people to reveal too much. I preferred it that way. Until now. Because I'd give anything to discover what made Tanner tick.

'If Remy hasn't revealed much to you, maybe Tanner will?' Makayla's exaggerated wink made me laugh. 'Don't you love that whole bad-boy thing he has going on?'

'Yeah, he's hot.' I settled for a smidgeon of honesty so Makayla wouldn't think anything was wrong.

Like exactly how much Tanner had revealed to me, and how much I'd liked it.

Makayla blew a raspberry. 'Queen of the understatement.'

'What do you want me to say? That he's so damn sexy I get hot flushes just thinking about him?' I pretended to fan my face and Makayla grinned.

'That's more like it…' She trailed off, as if unsure how to continue. 'I've got a confession to make.'

For an awful moment I wondered if Makayla had slept with Tanner too. The thought made bile rise in my throat and I swallowed, feeling increasingly foolish.

Of course a guy like him would go for a girl like Makayla. She was a bombshell. Not to mention beautiful inside and out.

'What's up?' I tried to fake nonchalance. It didn't work when my voice came out a tad high.

Makayla screwed up her nose, but she couldn't hide the twinkle in her eyes. 'I saw you. Last night. Heading into the VIP room with Hot Stuff.'

I exhaled in relief, unaware I'd been holding my breath.

'So you've been fishing for information this whole time?'

'Gotcha.' Makayla made a mock gun with her thumb and forefinger and fired it. 'Come on, sweetie, 'fess up. Did anything happen between you two?'

I'd never had a best friend. The girls at my private school had been bitches, students at uni in the few years I attended were aloof and Bardley's friends were as bland and boring as him.

In the few months I'd known Makayla I liked talking to her. Liked the way she breezed through life. Liked her exuberance and warmth and genuine enthusiasm for everything.

I could lie to her. Fob her off with some lame-ass vague response.

Instead, I found myself nodding, liking having a female confidante for once. 'We hooked up.'

Makayla squealed and jumped up and down. 'Hooked up as in kissed? Or hooked up as in—' She made lewd bumping gestures with her hands.

'Yeah, that.' I felt heat flush my cheeks. 'But you can't say a thing, okay?'

'Good for you, girlfriend.' She made a zipping motion over her lips, but her silence lasted all of two seconds as she eyed me with obvious admiration. 'The quiet ones are always the worst.'

Considering how I'd screamed the place down last night, I wasn't so quiet.

Makayla slugged me on the arm. 'I want details.'

I shook my head, not willing to divulge anything more. I didn't want Makayla casting sideways knowing glances at Tanner and I sure as hell didn't want him thinking I couldn't keep my mouth shut.

I'd never been the type to blab my personal business and I wasn't about to start now. 'Sorry. I don't kiss and tell.'

'Fair enough.' Makayla sighed, her grin goofy. 'I'm happy for you, sweetie. You deserve to have a little fun. But if he has a brother other than Remy, let me know.'

She made a downward sign with her thumb. 'I'm in a major slump. Both professionally and romantically. I've attended eight auditions in the last fortnight, nada. And my dating average is less than that.'

'Those stage shows must be nuts not to hire you,' I said, defending my friend when in fact I had no idea how good a dancer she was. Sure, she could burn up the dance floor with her disco moves but professionally I didn't know how she performed. 'As for guys, most of them have rocks in their heads, but you're gorgeous and sweet. You'll find a good one soon.'

A surprisingly vulnerable smile tugged at the corners of her mouth. 'Hope you're right, because I don't do so well when I'm in a drought.' She wiggled her eyebrows suggestively. 'I need a good man between my legs offstage so I can use my legs to create great dance moves onstage.'

'Maybe that's the problem? You're after a good man when what you need is a bad man?'

We laughed and I impulsively leaned over to hug her. 'Thanks for taking me out last night. I needed it.'

'The dancing or the bad guy between your legs?'

'Both,' I said, my naughty grin matching Makayla's. 'Now, if you're done interrogating me, can we lock up so I can catch up on some sleep?'

'Sure,' she said, pushing off the bench. 'So he kept you up all night, huh?'

'And then some.'

The way Tanner had touched me, stroked me, caressed me—*everywhere*—had blown my mind. I'd never imagined sex could be so good. He'd driven me to the brink so many times, teasing and tasting, before pushing me over with a skill that spoke of years of practice.

I should've felt jealous at the thought of him using his mastery on countless women in the past. Instead, all I could feel was grateful. Very, very grateful.

'Come on, let's close up before I begin to hate you.' Makayla smiled and bumped me with her hip. 'And a word of advice? Don't overthink things with Hot Stuff. He's not here for long, so you should be in this for a good time.'

Whatever 'this' was. Because right now I didn't have a freaking clue. I'd labelled last night as a one-night stand. But from what I'd read in magazines, you didn't usually have to see your one-night stand again. Me, I'd have Tanner in my face for the next few weeks.

Was I really that good an actress that I could pretend nothing had happened and erase the memories of him licking me all over?

Worse, did I want to?

I throbbed just thinking about what we'd done last night. How much stronger would the urge to jump him be when he was standing in front of me?

Did I have the willpower to resist another shot at achieving mind-blowing pleasure?

With the prospect of Tanner showing up for work tomorrow, guess I'd soon find out.

CHAPTER TEN

Tanner

I KNEW THE second I opened my eyes she was gone.

I should've been ecstatic. I never let women stay over. In fact, I rarely brought women here. Over the years I'd been in Sydney I could count the number of dates I'd brought to my penthouse on one hand.

Then again, Abby hadn't been a date.

She'd been…what? A one-night stand? A chance hook-up? A goddamn mistake? Technically, all of the above, which begged the question: Why the hell did I feel so disgruntled to find her gone?

That was another thing. I'd slept better last night than I had in years. Usually I liked the bed all to myself, hated having anyone encroach on my personal space. Yet after the fifth time we'd fucked she'd spooned me and I'd liked it, to the point I'd fallen into a deep slumber, so deep I hadn't heard her leave.

Shit. Why did she have to sneak out of here like some damn fugitive?

Peeved, I pushed out of bed and headed for the shower. Alone, when I'd had grand plans for the two of us in my expansive double shower complete with rain head and angled jets. Lots of possibilities with those jets. Especially with how responsive she'd been... I could've turned her to face the back wall, where she would've braced. I could've bent her forward. Adjusted the jets to hit her sweet spot. Taken her from behind...

Swearing, I turned the taps to cold. Ice cold. Jerking off wouldn't ease the desire pounding through my veins like the insistent beat of a drum. Burying myself in Abby would, but that wasn't an option. Not now. Probably not ever again.

Last night had been an aberration. It had to be.

I'd vowed to not touch Remy's protégé but that had shot to shit when she'd come on to me like an eager virgin. I should've had stronger willpower. I hadn't. Not getting laid for months had short-circuited my brain. Both the big and little one.

A lousy excuse because I could've stopped her. I should've stopped her. But I hadn't, and now I had to live with the consequences.

Namely seeing her every day at work and keeping my hands off her.

I wasn't a complete idiot. I knew we couldn't have a repeat. That would be a disaster of monumental proportions.

Women like Abby didn't do one-night stands. They did romance and bouquets and all that crap, no matter how much they protested to the contrary. Especially if she hadn't been with a guy in a year.

That blew me away. How could a beautiful woman who'd come out of a shitty marriage not have wanted to purge her past? Then again, maybe her ex had done such a number on her that she'd sworn off men for a while? Whatever the reason, I'd been the beneficiary, because the way she'd reacted to my every touch had blown my mind.

That was what had me rattled the most. The flashbacks of what we'd done. Her on her front, me entering her from behind. Her with her legs spread, me eating her out. Her riding me like a cowgirl. Her clawing my back and biting my shoulder and tentatively licking my cock like it was the best damn popsicle she'd ever tasted.

'Fuck,' I muttered, towelling off and dressing in record time.

I couldn't go to the patisserie, not today. Couldn't face her. Not without my every erotic thought replaying like an X-rated flick on constant repeat.

She'd know. Then where would we be?

If my willpower had been at an all-time low last night, now that I knew how combustible we were between the sheets, would I be able to resist? Doubtful. Which meant I needed time and space between us to gain perspective.

That meant staying away from Le Miel.

I grabbed a bottled banana smoothie from the fridge and headed out. There'd been a shitload of work I could've done at Embue last night before I got distracted. In the best possible way. The way she'd come on to me in my private room…

Damn, I better hole away in my office and stay clear of that room. Having wavering willpower was one thing. Deliberately putting myself into a fraught situation another.

I'd try to do the right thing where Abby was concerned but I wasn't a saint, and I knew that keeping her at arm's length until Remy got back on his feet would slowly but surely kill me.

I arrived at Embue, parked in the private underground spot reserved for me and entered the club. All these years later it never failed to give me a thrill that I owned this place. That it flourished. That it continued to grow.

Despite dear old Dad's many dire predictions I'd never amount to anything.

How many times had I listened to his snide comments, berating me, battering my self-esteem, while he deliberately praised Remy when he wasn't around, knowing it would make me feel like shit? How many times had he served me the crusts off the fresh bread loaf while he got the thickest slices? How many times had he given me a shrivelled chicken wing while he ate the juicy breast?

After Mum died, on the rare occasions Remy was home he thought Dad was a mean prick too, but he'd excused his mood swings and anger as grief. But I knew better because Dad saved his own special brand of vitriol for me alone.

Even before Mum had died, I'd felt unworthy. That I was not good enough. That I couldn't do anything right. He treated me like a second-class citizen but only when Mum and Remy couldn't see.

I didn't get it. Had always thought it was my fault, some inherent flaw only Dad could see. Until the day Mum died and I overheard the final argument that drove her to her death. The day the old bastard revealed the truth behind his hatred and I'd vowed to never let his insults or shoddy treatment hurt me ever again.

Because it wasn't about me. It was about him. His ridiculous hang-ups and assumptions that had driven Mum to her death and driven me to be nothing like him.

I'd rejoiced the day the prick had died. I'd attended his funeral out of respect for my brother. Remy never understood my latent hatred of our father, and I'd never told him the truth. Better that one of us had good memories rather than none.

Then again, he'd been five years older than me and already holding down a part-time pastry chef apprenticeship while juggling school at fifteen, so he hadn't been around to witness Dad's ritualistic, systemic torture of me. The son he blamed for his entire miserable life.

It meant nothing now. He couldn't hurt me any more. But every time I strode through one of my clubs I saluted him for giving me the drive, the ambition, to be so much better than he ever gave me credit for.

'Hey, Tanner, didn't expect to see you today.' Hudson Watt, my manager and oldest friend, slapped me on the back as I entered the bar area. 'Aren't you meant to be making pastries or croissants or some other fancy-schmancy shit?'

'Had a stack of stuff I wanted to check up on last night but didn't get a chance so thought I'd spend the day here.'

Hudson grinned, the same smug grin he'd given me in high school when I'd tried to weasel out of a history assignment by devising an elaborate lie and he'd seen right through me.

'Bit busy last night, huh?' Hudson filled a glass with water and added a lime twist before sliding it along the bar towards me. 'Here. You're probably de-hydrated after swapping spit with that hot blonde you had holed away in your private VIP room.'

'What are you, twelve?' I downed the water any-way. 'I don't know what you're talking about.'

'Come on, man, don't spin me some line.' Hudson slugged me on the arm. 'I've seen you sweet-talk more girls out of their panties than the number of mojitos I've served. And considering I've worked here for ten years and filled in on many occasions, that's a shitload of mojitos.'

I chuckled. 'I was giving Abby the grand tour, then I took her home.'

'Her home or yours?'

I could've fobbed Hudson off but the guy was right. We'd been friends for a long time. If anyone knew me, faults and all, he did.

'Mine.' I pinched the bridge of my nose to ease some of the tension building behind my eyes. 'Should never have happened.'

Hudson's eyebrows shot up. 'That's the first time I've heard you express post-coital regret.'

'Bullshit. Remember that time we double-dated those bogan twins from Bundaberg? Disastrous.'

Hudson laughed. 'Don't change the subject. From what I saw, this Abby chick had class stamped all over her. Too cool between the sheets, huh?'

Too hot, more like it. Scorching, soul-searing hot. The type of woman who got inside a guy's head and wouldn't leave, no matter how hard I tried. And I'd tried. Boy, had I tried. But she was there, every time I allowed my attention to wander for a moment. Front and centre. Naked. Wanton. Willing.

Fuck.

'Abby's Remy's protégé and I shouldn't have gone there.'

'Why not?' Hudson's grin turned wicked. 'From the way I saw her draped all over you as you left this place as fast as humanly possible, she was seriously into you.'

'Still too complicated,' I said, shaking my head. 'Anyway, what's going on with you?'

'You don't get off that easy.' Hudson glanced at his watch. 'I was just heading down to Jim's for a quick workout before coming back here to do the books. Want to join me so I can grill you some more?'

'You're still working out at Jim's?'

That place had saved my life as a kid. I'd been fourteen when Hudson had taken me to the run-down gym on the outskirts of Kings Cross, where kids could box for recreation, sport or just to vent their frustration.

I'd done a lot of the latter.

When I couldn't tell anyone about Dad's crappy treatment at home, I'd take it out at Jim's. First on a punching bag, later in sparring matches with other teens. It had been cathartic, being able to physically vent in a safe place, and I hadn't been back in over a decade.

'Yeah, no better place to spar.' Hudson jabbed a left hook in my direction and feigned a dodge to the right. 'Come on, will do you good. You've drifted off about five times in the last few minutes and that means you've got it bad for this new chick.'

If he only knew. Being with Abby hadn't damp- ened my attraction to her. If anything it had intensified, and that wasn't a good thing. 'Don't you ever stop with the bullshit?'

Hudson chuckled and this time jabbed me on the arm for real. 'Let's go, champ. It'll be my pleasure to whip your ass.'

'Dream on, dickhead.'

An hour later, Hudson had done exactly that but I felt so much better for the workout and being at Jim's had a lot to do with my lift in mood.

Walking into Jim's was like coming home. The pungent smell of sweat warred with liniment. Four boxing rings flooded with natural light from rows of windows set high in the walls. Free weights and punching bags in the far corner, with an old-fashioned juice bar next to it.

There weren't many guys around this morning. Probably all at work. Where I should be, rather than running from my present into the past.

'You're rusty,' Hudson said, draping a towel around his neck and handing me one.

'And you're soft in the middle,' I said, socking a punch into his solar plexus. He dodged.

'Bet that's not what Abby says to you.'

This time, I aimed harder and he sidestepped easily, laughing so loud a trainer nearby grinned.

'Seriously, dude, if you like her this much, do something about it.'

I hated the flare of hope his words elicited. 'Like what, Einstein?'

'Damned if I know. Do I look like an expert on women?'

'Good point.' I wiped the sweat off my face and towelled my torso. 'Seeing anyone?'

'Nah. Between managing the bar and doing part-time work at the theatre, I don't have much time left for a relationship.'

'Who said anything about the R word?'

He snorted. 'I'm not like you. I like to date women for longer than five hours.'

'I'll have you know Abby stayed the night.'

The second the retort popped out I wished I could take it back.

'And there you go, dude. Proof that she's not like the rest.'

'Back off, bozo.' I advanced on him in mock anger so he'd do just that.

Predictably, Hudson just stood there like the big, blond lug he'd always been. Loyal to a fault. The kind of mate I could depend on.

'Make me, squirt.'

Considering I towered over him by three inches, it was a hollow taunt, one he'd made many times as a kid, and we laughed.

'Let's get back to the club and you can show me proof you haven't been embezzling me out of a fortune.' I tugged on the end of a glove lace with my teeth, thinking I should do this more often.

Boxing worked off frustration of all varieties, including sexual, like nothing else could.

'Sounds like a plan.' As Hudson took off his gloves and helped me with mine, I knew he wanted to say more but was holding back.

'What's up?'

'It's this place.' Hudson gestured around. 'I don't get back here as often as I like but whenever I do it's like the past crashes over me and I wonder why I put myself through it.'

That was another thing that had bonded us, our crappy childhoods. His father had made mine look like a frigging saint.

'Cut the heartstring crap, bozo, and let's get back to work.'

Hudson blinked rapidly, as if coming back from a place of bad memories, before his signature grin made me sigh in relief. 'After you, big guy.'

As we traded banter while changing, swapping the usual crap guys did, I knew I'd done the right thing in taking time away from the patisserie and Abby today.

But I couldn't play chicken for ever, and come to-morrow I'd be back there, wishing I hadn't complicated matters and wanting her more than ever.

CHAPTER ELEVEN

Abby

AFTER MAKAYLA AND I locked up I'd intended on taking a hot bath and having an early night. But as I entered the small one-room apartment over the patisserie, it didn't offer the comfort it usually did.

I'd never forget the first time Remy brought me up here and said I could stay as long as I liked. That had been over a year ago, the day I'd walked out on Bardley and into Le Miel. In search of comfort via the delicious pastries Remy made, I'd frequented the patisserie often during my marriage, using it as my go-to place to escape home. I'd spent many afternoons sitting at the small table near the counter, sipping at a latte and trying to stop at only one croissant while studying.

Remy would come out from the kitchen occasionally and he'd always stop to chat. As kind-hearted and generous with his time as he was with his magnificent pastries.

I'd never plucked up the courage to tell him that I also enjoyed baking and that to me he had my dream job. Instead, when he asked, I pretended to wax lyri-

cal about my business degree and how happy I was
juggling university with marriage.

If he saw through my brittle smile, he never said;
that was the kind of man he was. And that fateful day
when I'd found my backbone and had the guts to walk
away from Bardley, he still hadn't prodded for information despite me coming in here like I had a pack
of wolves on my tail.

On impulse, I'd asked him for a job and once he'd
heard my sob story he'd offered me the apartment too.

I'd taken one look at the cosy, light-filled space and
fallen in love. Pockmarked mahogany floorboards
covered in rugs in the most vibrant peacock blues and
crimsons, a faded chintz sofa and chairs, a bookcase
overflowing with classics and a kitchenette stocked
with everything I'd need to whip up healthy meals
for one.

The small bedroom and bathroom had been basic
but I hadn't cared. I'd never lived on my own, moving straight from my parents' Double Bay mansion
into Bardley's Vaucluse monstrosity gifted to him by
his folks when we married. Having the freedom to
do whatever I liked in my own space had been heady
stuff for a girl like me.

So I'd moved in with the few suitcases I'd packed
when I'd walked away from my marriage, had paid
Remy six months' rent in advance—a pittance, really,
considering the rental prices in this upmarket part of
town—and settled into a routine.

Living the life I wanted.

But today, restlessness plagued me and after I'd
done a quick circuit or ten of the apartment I decided
to go for a drive. Another thing I liked doing that I'd

never had much of a chance to do in my past: driving for leisure.

Dad had a chauffeur that had dropped me at school and picked me up, and Bardley roared around in his sports car when he wasn't getting a private car to ferry him around. My narrow-minded husband had never understood my love of driving, had mocked me endlessly for wanting to drive out of the city on a weekend with no destination in my mind.

So I'd rarely done it; hadn't been worth the angst. Besides, it had been difficult to squirrel away any me-time when Bardley demanded I keep up with his hectic social schedule and attend every boring polo party/sailing regatta/race carnival as his arm candy.

These days, on my limited down time, I drove for the heck of it. For the pleasure of exploring new places. For the simple fact I could, without anyone telling me I was an idiot or worse.

It wasn't until I was in my hatchback and cruising the streets did I realise where I was heading.

Home.

Not the harbourside mansion I'd lived in for twenty-one years before I got married, but the suburb. Ritzy Double Bay. Everything seemed brighter here, like a fairy had sprinkled glitter over the entire suburb.

I drove aimlessly along the lush tree-lined boulevards, passing row upon row of incredible palatial homes with manicured emerald lawns, tennis courts and pool houses that could house a large family.

Trendy boutiques I'd frequented when I didn't baulk at the four-figure price tag on a pair of shoes or hold back when signing up for the newest release designer handbag.

Cafés I'd regularly met my friends at, to do nothing but chat about our caviar facials and the latest celebrity break-up. Friends that hadn't given a crap when I'd left Bardley. Friends that hadn't even called.

Past Redleaf Beach, a gorgeous slice of Sydney Harbour foreshore, where I'd sat on the sand for hours sometimes, wishing I could swim like the bathers doing laps in the tidal enclosure but too afraid to bring it up in case Bardley ridiculed me for wanting to learn how to swim at my age and conquer my fear of deep water.

I gripped the steering wheel tighter as I glimpsed a sprawling whitewashed building fringed in lush gardens. The day spa Mum and I used to attend.

Emotion clogged my throat as I homed in on the elaborate gold-embossed entrance, wondering what I'd do if I glimpsed Mum. But she was nowhere in sight and I found myself pulling into a parking spot and killing the engine.

Crazy, as even if I saw her I wouldn't approach her. Not when a hotbed of resentment and hurt festered inside me that not once over the last twelve months had she contacted me. Other than those fraught initial phone calls when she'd begged me to reconsider walking out on my marriage.

Phone calls where she hadn't asked how I was or where I was living or what I was doing to support myself since I'd been cut off financially from Bardley and my folks. Oh, no. Mum's phone calls consisted of cajoling alternating with berating.

'How could you be so stupid, darling? Walking away from your husband? Your home? Your friends?'

'What were you thinking, leaving behind a life of luxury?'

'You've embarrassed your husband and you've mortified us. Return home immediately!'

The latter had been the most laughable because I hadn't had a home with Bardley. Not really. We'd been friends coexisting in a massive house. More like housemates, really, who had lacklustre sex on occasion.

Not that anyone besides us knew the truth. To our friends and family we were the luckiest couple in Australia. Married young. The successful merging of two powerhouse families. A glamorous life filled with the best money could buy, with a fortune guaranteed to keep our offspring in the lap of luxury.

The biggest sham ever perpetuated.

I hated myself for putting up with it for so long. For being a mousy, subservient girl who went along with whatever my parents wanted, including marrying a man I only felt a lukewarm affection for.

I'd allowed myself to get caught up in the euphoria of having some guy pay me attention. Because that was what Bardley had done, wooed me with the express purpose of marriage, as his folks had suggested to him.

While he'd had dollar signs in his eyes, envisaging a family merger that would consolidate fortunes, I'd had stars in my eyes, naively hoping that marriage would provide the excitement I'd been craving.

Instead, Bardley had morphed into the dweeb I'd always suspected he was, with a mean streak that flourished once he had a ring on my finger. And I'd started to lose myself, piece by piece, becoming a listless yes-person who'd do anything to keep the peace and not earn his wrath.

What a fool.

I'd hated being that spineless, mouthless idiot and as I stared at the day spa and watched a mother and daughter exit, heads close together as they gossiped, their blond-streaked hair shiny in the lights flickering on, I realised maybe I didn't miss my old life so much after all.

I couldn't fathom my parents' lack of contact, their complete lack of interest in my well-being now that I wasn't doing what they wanted.

Dad had always been aloof and business-focussed, so I didn't expect as much from him. The only time he'd ever paid me attention—Mum too, for that matter—was when we did something that pleased him. Otherwise, he'd convey his displeasure through angry silences that lasted for days, ensuring that I learned from a young age to make him happy.

So it didn't surprise me that he hadn't contacted me, but for Mum to ignore me too…it hurt. A lot.

I'd rung twice over the last six months, more to touch base and hear a familiar voice. The maid had skilfully diverted my call both times, so I never got to speak to my folks.

They hadn't returned my calls.

Was I stupid to still miss them? To still hold onto a faint hope they'd eventually come around? Maybe, but they were my parents and no matter how crappy their treatment, a small part of me wished they'd understand one day.

A tear plopped onto my forearm, startling me. I hadn't realised I'd been crying. Swiping a hand across my eyes, I shot the day spa a final wistful glance before starting the engine.

I should be happy. Last night with Tanner had purged my past once and for all. I should be rejoicing. Instead, I couldn't help but wish I could have my old life mix successfully with my new.

At least the drive had achieved one objective.

Forget Tanner.

But as I headed back to Le Miel, knowing I'd have to confront him all too soon, maybe this new life I'd craved so much was a lot more than I'd bargained for.

CHAPTER TWELVE

Tanner

'FLOUR STOCKS ARE LOW—same with sugar and butter. We've got a flood of orders coming in that haven't been catalogued. And the front display cabinet looks like something a toddler arranged. What the hell's going on?'

I glowered at Abby, hating the flicker of resentment in those stunning blue eyes that had been filled with passion only two days ago.

I'd been riding her—metaphorically, worse luck—ever since I'd arrived at seven this morning. But I had to keep it up, had to keep emotional distance between us, otherwise I wouldn't be able to keep my hands off her.

Walking in this morning and having her fix me with that cool blue indifferent gaze, like nothing had happened between us, made me want to bend her over the counter and thrust into her until sweet, sensual Abby was back.

I liked that Abby. Liked her willing and wanton and wet. Desperate for me.

But I liked that Abby too much—too much to be good for me—and therein lay the problem.

So I'd donned my poker face and reflected her indifference right back at her. Though it was an act. A forced act we were both perpetuating in the hope neither of us would crack.

I'd known it would be like this. That she would pretend like nothing had happened. Hell, she'd made it painfully obvious she didn't want me ever since we'd met, her disdain palpable. Which only served to dent my ego and make me want to rattle her all the more.

It was like some weird twisted game we were playing. Push and pull. A battle of wills. Too bad for her, I'd never backed down from a challenge in my life. I could out-stubborn a donkey. Because I'd learned from an early age that the only way to cope with Dad's derogatory crap was with indifference.

He'd hated it. I'd done it more. He'd never made me crack. Nobody could. I'd become too hardened, too cynical, too tough.

Too tough for the likes of Abby, that was for sure.

I'd ultimately break her and that wouldn't be good. For her, for Remy, maybe for me too.

Though I was a big boy, I could take it. But Remy would hate me for running off his golden girl and I couldn't let that happen. I didn't care what other people thought of me. Anyone except Remy. His opinion mattered. He mattered. He always had.

So I'd keep up this ridiculous charade no matter how much I wanted Abby.

'I'll get Makayla to check the orders and the front display. As for supplies, today's delivery is late. It happens sometimes.' She glared at me like something she'd stepped in. A particularly nasty something that stuck to her shoe no matter how hard she tried to wipe it off. 'I'll go check in the storeroom. We usually stock extras for emergencies.'

'Fine,' I muttered through gritted teeth, feeling like an ogre as I watched her retreating back and her ass.

I couldn't help it. Remembering the soft curve of her cheeks. The way they felt beneath my hands. How she'd squealed when I'd bitten her.

She paused at the door to the storeroom and glanced over her shoulder.

Damn, sprung, as I dragged my gaze upward but not fast enough.

With a raised eyebrow, she said, 'If your foul mood is a result of what happened between us and you're feeling awkward, forget it.' Her gaze turned glacial. 'I have.'

I wouldn't have been surprised if she'd flipped me the bird as she stalked into the storeroom and slammed the door.

'Fuck.' I dragged a hand through my hair and re-sisted the urge to kick the nearest counter.

I should leave her to her snit in peace. But that was the thing about never backing down; I couldn't stop my feet from following her even if I wanted to. And I didn't. I wanted her to take back that last remark.

She hadn't forgotten our steamy encounter any more than I had. So she must've thrown it out there in hurt.

And I hadn't wanted to hurt her.

I'd apologise for acting like a jackass. Smooth the way towards a better working relationship. Yeah, that was the plan.

A plan that imploded the moment I entered the storeroom and saw her braced against a table, chest heaving, eyes flashing, chin tilted up in defiance.

'Get out,' she yelled, her hands balling into fists, and she thumped the table.

In response, I kicked the door shut.

Locked it.

'Don't you dare come near me,' she said, not moving a muscle as I advanced on her. She squared her shoulders the closer I got, staring me down. Even when we stood almost toe to toe, she didn't flinch. 'You're a boorish, idiotic, moody—'

My mouth slammed onto hers. Our teeth clashed a little, our noses bumped. A disastrous kiss from an experienced guy like me but I didn't care. I didn't care about anything but savouring the sweetness of her mouth again. Taunting her tongue to match mine. Exploring the crevices of her mouth like I'd never get enough.

Her hands clutched at my shirt, like she wanted to push me away. She hauled me closer, clawing at the cotton, wanting skin.

I knew the feeling.

At my apartment two nights ago, I'd worshipped her body. Taken my time. A leisurely exploration that had imprinted on my brain. Every dip and curve. Every ticklish spot. Every erogenous inch that I'd licked and stroked and caressed until she'd been mindless with want.

Now there was no time for finesse.

'Hurry up,' she growled in my ear, nipping at the tender skin below it, her teeth grazing my skin with short, sharp nibbles before she licked her way along my jaw towards my mouth.

Sensual Abby was back and I couldn't be happier.

I made short work of her zipper. Pushed her panties down. And slid my finger into moist heat.

'More,' she murmured, and I was only too happy to acquiesce to her demand.

I fished a condom out of my wallet, unzipped and sheathed myself in record time.

I had to be inside her. Now.

With her pants around her ankles, I couldn't spread her legs wide so I spun her around and bent her over the table.

Exposing that gorgeous ass.

'You like doing it doggy style, don't you?' I slid a hand around the front, fingering her clit as I nudged at her slick folds. 'Two times the other night.'

'Too much talking.' She glanced over her shoulder, her eyes flashing indigo fire, taunting me.

I entered her in a smooth thrust that made her gasp.

'Better?' I whispered, leaning over her, making our fit even snugger.

She moaned in response and wiggled her ass.

She wanted more? I'd give it to her.

I slid in and out. Slow at first. Wanting to drive her as mad as she drove me. But I couldn't hang on. Not when I'd been fantasising about this for the last two days. Not when she felt better than I remembered.

My cock pulsed with every thrust, the pressure building, and my finger picked up tempo on her clit until she was pushing back at me as hard as I was pushing into her.

'So good...' She stiffened, a moment before she

let out a long, satisfied groan, as her pussy clenched around me.

I came so hard I saw spots.

This time, when she glanced over her shoulder at me, her smile was smug. Satisfied. I knew the feeling.

'Hope that puts you in a better mood,' she said, straightening a little so I had no option but to pull out and take care of business.

'We shouldn't have done that.'

I knew it had been the wrong thing to say when her face fell, but she masked it quickly with a fake smile I was growing to hate.

'Seems like we shouldn't do a lot of things that are bad for us, like eating leftover croissants, but we do it anyway.'

She sounded flippant but I heard the hurt lacing her words.

Damn, I'd done it again. Caused her pain when it was never my intention.

'Look, we need to talk this out—'

'From where I'm standing, there wasn't much talking involved, just the way I wanted it.' She pulled up her pants and zipped up, elegant and nonchalant, whereas I felt gauche doing the same thing. 'We don't need to talk about anything.'

She spun away from me and I grabbed her hand, tugging her back to face me. 'I've handled this badly and I'm sorry. But we do have to work this out, Abby, otherwise it's going to be a tough few weeks.'

To her credit, she eyeballed me, trying to stare me down. 'What are you really sorry for? Being a douche the whole day or not being able to keep your hands off me?'

She packed a punch. I liked that. Liked straight shooting.

'Both.'

To my relief, I saw the corners of her mouth twitch. A mouth I remembered doing wicked things to me a few nights ago and just like that I was hard again, ready and raring to go.

'You don't have to apologise for the…sex.' Damn, she was cute when she blushed. 'I like it. In fact, I think we should keep doing it.'

'Pardon me?'

I could've sworn she'd just said we should keep having sex. Nice in practice, terrible in theory.

'A fling. Short term. No strings.' She eased her hand out of mine before I could react. 'It'll be good for me. Purging my past once and for all.'

Bitterness made my jaw clench. So that was all I was. A fuckable solution to her yearlong celibacy. A way to get back on the proverbial horse. I should be flattered. Instead, all I could think was how I'd never been good enough growing up and I wasn't good enough now for anything more than a short-term fling.

Every guy's dream, having a woman articulate no-strings sex. In reality, how often did it turn out that way? Women tended to want more. More emotion. More commitment. More.

But Abby seemed different. She hadn't been mooning around all day. She'd been nonchalant. All business. Like she didn't give a shit I'd been a grouchy ogre determined to keep her at bay.

So maybe she meant it when she said a no-strings fling. I should be ecstatic. Instead, I couldn't help but feel like yet again I'd come up short somehow. A hollow, empty feeling I'd spent years trying to conquer courtesy of dear old Dad's shabby treatment.

'So I'd be your walk on the wild side? Slumming it before you head back to the real world?'

Guilt shifted in her gaze before she shook her head. 'We're very different, so, yeah, part of the appeal is that bad-boy edge you've got going on. But I like you.' Her blush was back, staining her cheeks a vivid pink. 'I never knew sex could be that good, so call me greedy but I want more.'

Defiant, she took a step towards me and placed her hand on my chest. 'A lot more.'

I gritted my teeth against the urge to bend her over the table again. 'Just sex. No muss, no fuss?'

'I'm not a muss, fuss kind of girl.' She lowered her hand, using it to gesture around the storeroom. 'This place is my life. I want to complete my apprenticeship, become fully qualified, gain as much experience as I can with your brother, save like the devil and hopefully have my own patisserie one day. So you and me? A side benefit I'd never anticipated, but no way would I let it interfere with my dream.'

'Fair enough.'

She'd said all the right things. Talked the talk. But when it came to ending things, would she walk the walk?

'What about Remy?'

Confusion creased her brow. 'What about him?'

'My brother will bust my balls for tangling with you.'

'Does he have to know?'

'We don't bullshit each other. He's always had my back and I owe him.'

Damn, why had I spilled that? I should keep my distance. Sex, I could handle, but there was something about Abby that snuck beneath my defences and made me want to confide. Disconcerting when I'd never told anyone the truth, not even Remy.

Another side effect of putting up with Dad's shit for so long: I was ashamed. Ashamed of who I was around him, ashamed of the years I'd tolerated his crap, ashamed at the possibility of anyone ever finding out how much of a goddamn coward I'd been.

'I admire your loyalty.' She tilted her head, studying me with that penetrating stare that made me squirm a little. 'Family should stick together.'

The slight quiver in her voice, underlined with a healthy dose of vulnerability, slayed me. 'What about you? Any siblings?'

'No.'

One syllable laced with unspoken pain.

'Hence my parents' high expectations of me. Which also explains why they cut me off the first and only time I went against their wishes.' Her harsh laugh was devoid of amusement. 'Didn't matter that I didn't want a princess party as a ten-year-old. Or a formal ball for my sixteenth. Or to do a business degree.' Her breath hitched. 'Or to marry a guy more a friend at twenty-one. I always did the right thing. The expected thing. Until I walked away.'

She cleared her throat. 'I envy you your bond with Remy.'

'Don't ever envy me,' I said, sounding gruff. 'Remy and I are close from necessity.'

Curiosity sparked her eyes. 'What does that mean?'

Shit. There I went again, giving away too much.

'Nothing.' I made a big show of glancing at my watch. 'We need to get back out there.'

Other women would've badgered me for answers. Thankfully, Abby had more class. Or she really was serious about keeping things between us strictly physical.

'You're right.' She hesitated, a shy smile making something in my chest twang. 'After we finish work, do you want to come up to my apartment? I make a mean fettuccini carbonara.'

I should say no. Because Abby wasn't just inviting me up for pasta and we both knew it. But she'd been honest in asking for what she wanted, blunt in outlining the terms. Considering how much of a jackass I'd been today, dealing with my rampaging lust for her and not being able to have her, I'd be better off agreeing to her very adult arrangement than having another few frustration-filled weeks.

'I am partial to pasta.' I stepped in close and rested my hand on her waist, my thumb strumming the sliver of bare skin beneath her pants and shirt. 'And you.'

'Good. Glad that's settled.' She kissed me on the cheek, a surprisingly sweet gesture that made my chest tighten again.

But as I unlocked the door and followed her back to the kitchen, I knew deep down that things between us were far from settled.

It scared the crap out of me.

CHAPTER THIRTEEN

Abby

THIS WAS CRAZY.

I wanted this.

I asked for it.

But as I flitted around the kitchen, ensuring the pasta had cooked *al dente*, grating Parmesan into a bowl and uncorking a Riesling, I knew that no matter how nonchalant I acted about inviting a gorgeous guy up to my apartment, inside I was a hot mess.

Tanner had agreed to a fling.

My ovaries were still leaping at the thought two hours later. Then he'd gone and revealed snippets of his past and I'd moved from viewing him as a fine piece of ass to a guy with a soul.

Okay, so that sounded shallow. I'd already known he had deeper layers behind that tattooed front, but when he'd told me about him and Remy being close out of necessity…the pain lacing his voice had slain me.

I'd wanted to wrap my arms around him, to offer comfort I had no right giving. But I'd seen the inner war he waged reflected in his eyes, a kind of personal agony I had no hope of understanding. So I'd changed the subject. Gone back to work. And begged off thirty minutes early to shower and get dinner prepped.

I hadn't dated as a teen. Bardley had been my first in every way: first boyfriend, first lover, first partner I'd lived with. He hadn't appreciated my cooking, had always mocked my 'homebody tendencies'. He'd preferred to eat out at Sydney's finest restaurants, or get high-end catering in. So after the first week of married life I'd given up in the kitchen and grown increasingly despondent because of it.

Whenever I'd been unable to stay away from the kitchen and indulged my penchant for baking, he'd made snide comments and warned me not to eat any of that 'carb-filled crap' in case I got fat.

I should've bashed him over the head with a skillet when I had the chance.

I'd never really had the pleasure of cooking for a guy I fancied before: a guy who'd want me for dessert rather than the lemon tartlets I'd snaffled from downstairs. In fact, as I dished up the pasta and laid the large serving platter on the table, arranging the salad and Parmesan around it, I wondered if we'd even make it through the main course.

What had happened in the storeroom…indicative of why I'd proposed this fling in the first place. We'd been dancing around each other all day and I'd known his foul mood had been more to do with himself trying to maintain his distance than anything else.

So I'd challenged him, hoping he'd snap. Because working alongside Tanner after that sizzling night we'd spent together was pure torture. Having him brush past me, inhaling his manly scent tinged with citrus, feeling the heat radiating off him, watching those strong hands wrangling a dodgy oven door... I'd been hyperaware of him all day.

And craving him like I'd never craved anything in my entire life.

I'd never been the type of person to want things. I guess having everything I ever needed handed to me on a silver platter did that to a girl. I'd taken it for granted, being spoiled and indulged, even if I didn't ask for it.

So wanting Tanner with every cell in my body was new and I'd handled it as best I could: by throwing myself into work and baking like a maniac. Fulfilling every order for the day and then some, Le Miel's front display overflowing with my signature almond croissants, *bugnes* and *chaussons aux pommes*.

We'd sold out as usual, rarely able to keep up with demand, but today we'd only turned away two people near closing rather than the usual thirty. I'd been high on my success of coping without Remy when Tanner had taunted me, spoiling for a fight. So I'd given him one. Knowing he wouldn't back down and would follow me into the storeroom. Where he'd snapped.

I throbbed at the memory, pressed my hands between my legs to stem the insistent wanting. It didn't work and I knew that when he knocked on the door at any moment, I'd probably launch myself at him.

That was the thing with having average, infrequent sex. When you got the real thing, you were insatiable. We'd done it five times that night we'd spent together, and once today, yet having him inside me was all I could think about. Fantasising about the next time. And the time after that.

I'd turned into a man.

A loud knock made me jump and my palms instantly grew clammy. I swiped them down the sides of the simple cotton dress I'd changed into, wiggled my fingers and shook my arms out. Like a prize fighter warming up for a strenuous bout.

A bout of steamy, sizzling sex, if I had my way.

Anticipation made my body zing as I took my time answering the door.

Yeah, like playing hard to get would work now.

When I opened it, my breath caught. He'd ditched the long-sleeve shirt he'd been working in all day and wore a fitted white T-shirt that outlined every ridge of his muscular body. I could see the faintest outline of the tattoos beneath, tattoos I'd barely studied and wanted to learn in intricate detail. His shoulders stretched the cotton and, with his hands thrust into his pockets, his biceps bulged nicely.

I tried not to stare. It wasn't polite. But as I started at his broad shoulders and worked my way down, I couldn't look away. When I reached his jeans' pockets, and noted the sizeable bulge between, my mouth went dry.

I swallowed, trying to think of something witty to say, something that didn't sound like, 'Take me now.'

'Something smells good,' he said, stepping forward to fill my doorway when all I could think about was him filling me. He lowered his head to brush a barely there kiss on my cheek. 'The pasta too.'

'Come in,' I said, my voice sounding strangled as he stepped inside and I closed the door behind him. 'Hope you're hungry.'

'Ravenous.'

One simple word uttered in a low growl that made the hairs on the nape of my neck snap to attention and goosebumps pebble my skin.

My back sagged against the door as he braced his arms either side of me, pinning me. Like I wanted to move even if I could. He stared at me, his dark eyes glowing with intent and I knew in that instant I'd be reheating dinner later.

'Me too,' I squeaked out before launching myself at him.

He laughed and staggered back a step. I didn't care. I literally tried to climb him as I hooked a leg around his waist and grabbed at his shoulders. Needing him. Wanting him. Desperate for him.

He chuckled, his hands spanning my waist. 'We're not eating first?'

'We are,' I murmured, nipping his earlobe to show him exactly what I'd be feasting on. Him. Every delectable inch.

He groaned a little and, emboldened, I wondered how much more of him I could devour. While he'd gone down on me several delightful times the other night, I hadn't ventured near him with my mouth beyond a tentative lick or two, considering how large he was in my hand.

But tonight was about me taking what I wanted.

I wanted him.

I spun him around and pushed him up against the door. Tugged the hem of his T-shirt out of his jeans. Unsnapped them and lowered the zipper. Slid my way down so I knelt at his feet.

'What are you doing?' His voice was barely above a growl as he laid a hand on my head.

'Having an entree.' I flashed him my best cheeky smile, hoping to convey confidence when in fact I'd never given head before.

Bardley had found oral sex distasteful, so we'd never done it. I was glad. Made it all the more special doing it to a guy I really liked.

'Babe, you're killing me,' he said, his eyes round and slightly glazed as he watched me take him out of his jocks.

He was big and hard in my hand as I stroked from the base towards the head. Leaned forward to lick the tip. Awed by his size up close. Feeling completely out of my depth.

'Just so you know, I haven't done this before.'

His fingers tightened in my hair and I winced a little. 'What the—'

'So I may not be very good at it.'

He swore. 'Abby, whenever you touch me I combust, so whatever you do to me, sweetheart, is going to be frigging phenomenal.'

Emboldened by his confidence in me, I wrapped my lips around the head of his cock and sucked slightly. He swore again. Easing my lips over him, I licked. Swirled my tongue around. Savouring the velvet-soft skin covering steel, the faint muskiness of him.

I couldn't take him all the way in, he was too big, but as I slid my mouth up and down, sucking as I went, I started to get the hang of it. If the sounds Tanner made were any indication, he was enjoying it too.

'Babe, I need to be inside you. I need…ah fuck.' His hand fisted tighter in my hair as I picked up tempo, sucking like I couldn't get enough.

He came on a low groan that made me feel like a wanton goddess and I'd never felt so sexy.

I'd never understood the articles I'd read in magazines, where women raved about how much power they had over men in the bedroom. To me, kneeling in front of a guy getting him off with your mouth reeked of subservience. But giving pleasure to Tanner this way made me feel good in a way I hadn't anticipated: like I was capable of bringing a guy to his knees, like I could do anything.

When I stood, he stared at me like I'd given him the best gift ever.

'Not bad for a novice, huh?' I couldn't keep the smug grin off my face.

'Not bad?' He reached for me and hauled me against his chest. 'You are stupendous.'

I had no idea how long we stood there, my face buried against him, breathing in the addictive scent of him, him squeezing the life out of me, but the longer he held me the harder I found it to delineate between us being a physical fling and something more.

I didn't have much experience with men. I didn't know if this was normal or not. Bardley had never been a cuddler and Makayla said the guys she slept with were the same, though that had more to do with her kicking them out so they couldn't spend the night than anything else.

But the way Tanner hugged me now, like he never wanted to let go, made me feel…special.

A very dangerous feeling to have around this man.

I knew we were nothing beyond a mutual attraction. Two people thrown together at the right time, willing to slake a thirst.

But for the moment, wrapped in his arms, I found it difficult not to wish for more.

CHAPTER FOURTEEN

Tanner

'THIS IS CATEGORICALLY the best pasta I've ever tasted.'
I pushed away my empty plate with a contented sigh.
'You're an amazing cook.'

Abby flushed, her cheeks glowing the same pretty
pink they did after sex. 'Bet you say that to all the
girls.'

'Only the ones who give me great head before serving up a meal like this.'

She blushed harder but her eyes glittered with tri-
umph, like I'd paid her the best compliment ever. 'I'm
glad you liked it,' she said, her tone demure but those
damn eyes, big and blue and defiant, alerting me to
the fact she wasn't just talking about the pasta.

I liked this side of her. Bold and confident. Taunting and teasing. Allowing her inner flirt to come out
and play when I had a feeling she'd rarely done that
before.

To think, I'd been the lucky bastard to be on the
receiving end of her first blowjob. What kind of a
putz had her ex been, a frigging eunuch? How had

he not wanted to experience everything with this incredible woman?

Me, I wanted it all. I'd have it all. Taking her on an erotic journey she'd never forget.

I'd wanted to go down on her at the door, return the favour. But she'd sauntered off, citing the food was getting cold, and that we'd have plenty of time for that later.

I'd agreed because it heightened anticipation. And I hadn't been able to think straight with my mind reeling from the impact of coming in her mouth. I'd been hard throughout dinner and, while I hadn't lied about this being the best damn pasta I'd ever eaten, I wanted to eat her.

'Have you spoken with Remy today?'

Just like that, she doused my libido like she'd dumped cold water over me.

'Yeah, the docs are pleased with his progress, but he's itching to get back here.'

'Probably doesn't trust us,' she said, her lips curving in a mischievous smile. 'Considering what we've been up to, I guess he's right.'

'I'm going to visit him tomorrow.'

After what had happened in the storeroom, I'd already made up my mind to come clean. I couldn't lie to Remy. Anyone but him.

Then again, I'd been doing it to him for most of our lives. Before Mum had died, she'd been a buffer between Dad and me, so I'd only been exposed to his hatred a few times. But after she'd died and Dad's guilt and anger had coalesced into a hard ball of rage against me, I'd had to lie to Remy on the rare times I saw him at home.

I remembered those nights vividly, when he'd come home late after putting in extra hours at a bakery and have a mountain of homework to get through too. He'd ask how was my day, was I doing okay at school, then grab a snack and head into his room. He always bought my trite responses that everything was fine. If he'd picked up something was amiss, he probably put it down to me missing Mum.

He never, ever suspected the awful truth and I kept it that way. Remy was a good guy and I didn't want him feeling bad, even after the old bastard had curled up his toes and done us all a favour.

Something in my tone must've alerted her to my thoughts, because her smile faded. 'Are you going to tell him about us?'

I bit back my first response, 'there is no us', because that would irrevocably hurt her. Besides, there was an 'us' of sorts, even if labelling our insatiable craving for sex with each other was 'us'.

I nodded. 'He'll know if he asks me about you, which he will, and takes one look at my face.' I clasped my fingers in my lap to stop from fiddling with the edge of the tablecloth. 'In case you haven't noticed, I'm kinda goofy when it comes to you.'

Her smile softened the lines of concern bracketing her mouth. 'You know we're both consenting adults and what we do in our leisure time has nothing to do with him?'

'I know, but I don't like hiding something this important from him.'

Damn, it'd been the wrong thing to say, because she'd interpret me as saying our relationship was important when in fact I'd meant our involvement, being

Remy's brother and protégé, would be important to him. Yeah, that was what I'd meant. Right?

Thankfully, Abby didn't call me on it. 'If you two are that close, how come you haven't been around much the last year?'

'I travel a lot for work. Acting as a consultant for new clubs around the world takes time.'

It was a trite answer, a vague answer, and we both knew it.

'If you need to tell him, tell him,' she said, with a shrug. 'As long as he doesn't give you or me grief when it ends.'

I knew we had an expiration date. I was counting on it. I would never have started anything unless Abby knew it too. So why did the pasta feel like it had wedged in my chest, giving me a bad case of heartburn?

I pushed back from the table a little, clamping down on the urge to bolt while I still could. 'None of his business and as you said we're both consenting adults, so when this ends it won't be messy.'

I didn't buy her bright, fake smile for a second.

We were kidding ourselves.

No matter how often we articulated this was just physical and we could walk away clean at the end, the more time we spent together, the bigger the potential for fallout.

I should walk away now. Get the hell out before the sex morphed into something more.

But she stood at that moment and held out her hand. 'Ready for dessert?'

'We talking about those lemon tartlets I spied on the counter or something else?'

Her lips curved in naughtiness. 'I thought those tartlets would taste fabulous later.' She paused for effect as she leaned forward to murmur, 'In bed.'

I stood so fast my chair slammed against the wall. So much for making a run for it while I still could. Time to make a last-ditch stand so I could tell my conscience to shut the hell up later.

'When we first met, I had you pegged as some prissy, society princess playing at baking.'

An eyebrow quirked. 'And I had you pegged as a selfish, arrogant playboy who didn't give a crap about anyone but himself. Your point?'

'You may be a princess playing at baking but you're far from prissy.' My gaze boldly raked her body. 'And you're sensational in the sack.'

'Right back at you,' she said, with a haughty tilt of her head, playing up to my initial assessment. 'If you'd care to join me in the sack, maybe we can be sensational together?'

I hadn't put up much of a fight. Hell, it had been a token protest at best. But the time for backing out of this thing between us was long past. Whatever happened from here on in, I'd have to take full responsibility.

Because this was my call.

I knew it; she knew it.

She'd been upfront from the start, labelling me as a way to purge her past. But I hadn't returned the favour.

Because Abby was far more than just sex for me.

I was using her. In a way that would alienate her completely if she ever found out.

'Don't you back out on me now, Bad Boy.' She sauntered towards me, hooked her finger into my waistband and tugged. 'Whatever you're thinking, forget it. We're not invested in this emotionally, so stop second-guessing or feeling guilty or whatever it is you're doing, and come show me more of that beautiful body.'

I blew out a long breath, releasing some of the residual tension making my shoulders ache. 'I'd never have thought you'd be into tats.'

'They're incredible,' she said, tugging my T-shirt over my head and flinging it away. 'I could spend hours studying them.'

I didn't move as her fingertips skated over my skin, exploring, lingering, just as she had that first time in my private room at the club.

Now, like then, lust blinded me, pounding through my body in time with my heart.

I didn't get it. Abby was beautiful, but I'd dated stunning. She was inexperienced, where I'd dated sexpots who knew their way around a guy and then some. She blew hot and cold, whereas I'd been with women who were hot to trot any time of day or night.

But there was something about her that got under my skin in a way no woman ever had.

'What's your favourite?' My skin rippled with awareness as she paused over the four-leaf clover on my right shoulder blade.

And licked it.

'This one.'

'Why?'

'Because every time I see it, I get lucky.'

I laughed as she slid her arms around me from behind in an unexpected hug. 'I like it when you lose the frown.'

'I frown?'

'Quite a bit of the time,' she said, her breath fanning my back. 'It makes you look formidable, when you're really a pussycat.'

'Says who?'

'Me.' She released me and stepped around me, her eyes glowing with wicked intent. 'I think it's time you made me purr.'

I didn't have to be asked twice. Catching her by surprise, I scooped her into my arms and she squealed. Looped her arms around my neck. Proceeded to nip at my shoulder. Pleasurable bites that bordered on painful, accentuating the fine line we trod.

What we did now might feel good, but it had the potential to hurt like a bitch if it went pear-shaped.

I nudged open the door to her bedroom and strode inside, depositing her on the bed gently. She wanted to purr? I'd make sure of it.

'How did you know this was the bedroom?'

'I stayed here once, sleeping off a bender.' I undid my jeans, snagged a condom, and stepped out of them, along with my jocks.

Once again, her lack of curiosity surprised me. I'd half expected her to ask why I'd stayed here and not at Remy's house, why I'd turned up drunk at the patisserie in the first place. But she didn't say a word. Instead, she crooked her finger at me, shimmying up the bed to rest against the pillows.

'You are the most beautiful male I've ever seen.' She lay back, hands behind her head, studying me with unabashed appreciation. 'I could look at you all night.'

The longer she stared at me with shameless adoration, the better I felt. Like I could slay dragons for her. Like I could be the kind of guy she deserved.

But that was bullshit and the moment I thought it I knew I had to shatter this illusion. Because that was all it was. Something that appeared to be wonderful but could never be real.

I wasn't the guy for her. No matter how much I wished I was for this brief moment in time.

'And I could fuck you all night.'

If my crassness shocked her, she didn't show it. She just lay there, a smile playing about her mouth as her inquisitive gaze drifted from my chest, to my belly, to my cock.

'Then what are you waiting for?'

I started at her feet. Massaging her insteps. Tugging her toes. Drifting up to her ankles. Soft strokes that had her sighing with contentment and wriggling like a cut snake.

Holding onto her ankles, I tugged her down the bed a little. And spread her legs.

She wasn't wearing panties.

'Hot damn.' I crawled up the bed towards her, flipped the skirt of her dress up, baring her to me.

Slick folds glistening with how much she wanted me.

The feeling was entirely mutual.

'I love when you look at me,' she murmured, squirming a little when I slipped a finger inside her. 'You make me feel beautiful.'

'That's because you are, sweetheart.'

I slipped another finger in as my thumb found her clit, circling slowly as I watched her face. Shifting expressions of rapture and awe that made her eyes glow and her mouth go slack.

Maintaining eye contact, I lowered my head so I could feast on her. She loved this. I'd discovered that first-hand the other night. And giving her pleasure, no matter how fleeting, had become my number one priority.

I loved the sounds she made as I swept my tongue across her clit, through her folds, repeating the action over and over until she was panting and arching into me.

'Now.' She tempered her demand with a barely whispered 'Please.'

'Your wish is my command,' I said, lapping at her like I could never get enough.

She came hard, her hips lifting off the bed as she screamed my name.

'Lucky the patisserie cleared out an hour ago, otherwise we'd have customers queuing up outside your door to have what you're having.' I slid up the bed to lie next to her and slipped the straps of her dress off her shoulders. 'Maybe you should name the next decadent pastry you create a Screaming Orgasm?'

She mumbled something unintelligible as I peeled her dress off and flung it away, leaving her completely naked. Completely beautiful.

'What was that? You want another already?' I lazily circled a nipple before plucking it as it puckered. 'If you say so—'

'I want you inside me.' She stilled my hand, her gaze trying to convey a message I had no hope of comprehending.

It looked a lot like gratitude tinged with something

else, something I dared not label in case it scared the crap out of me. More than I already was.

'Done,' I said, sheathing myself and rolling her onto her side so we were face-to-face. 'I like a woman who knows what she wants and isn't afraid to ask for it.'

'And I like you,' she murmured, hooking her leg over my hip and sliding closer. 'Every inch of you.'

Not breaking eye contact, I slid into her in one smooth thrust and she sighed, the green flecks in her eyes sparking with mutual passion.

She felt so tight, so right, I knew I'd never forget this. Never forget her.

I needed to break eye contact, needed to stop her seeing into my soul, but as we rocked together slowly, sensually, I couldn't look away.

We didn't speak. No murmured dirty pleas. No naughty demands. Just the sound of our heavy breathing as we melded together.

Exquisitely slow. Deliciously drawn out.

Long, deep thrusts that made me mindless with wanting more.

As the first ripples of her orgasm clenched around me, I changed the angle of my hips a little, driving into her with enough force to make our heads bang.

'Oh, hell…' She came on a keen, the sexiest sound I'd ever heard as my balls tightened and I followed her over the edge a second later. Body taut. Mind blank. Stunned by the intensity of it and the ferocity of wanting to do it all over again as soon as humanly possible.

'More like heaven,' I said, disconcerted to find we still hadn't broken eye contact, and in that moment reality crashed over me.

What we'd done wasn't just sex.

We'd moved past that.

The intimacy, the eye contact, the yearning to stay inside her, all added up to one thing.

· Trouble.

CHAPTER FIFTEEN

Abby

I USUALLY STARTED baking at six most mornings.

Today I started at five.

Tanner had been snoring softly when I'd woken at four, giving me precious time to study him. A slumbering Tanner was nothing like awake Tanner.

Asleep, Tanner's face softened, making him look younger. Awake, tension bracketed his mouth and made his neck muscles bulge a little. Asleep, his lips relaxed into a semi-smile and his head lolled on the pillow all slack and cute.

It made me wonder, had he always been this uptight or had something happened to put him on alert at all times?

He'd dropped another hint about his childhood, about him and Remy, and while I'd never pry behind his back I couldn't help but wish Remy had spoken more about his younger brother.

I knew next to nothing about Tanner King and I'd been okay with that. Having mind-blowing sex with a guy for a short-term fling didn't demand shared confidences.

But last night had changed all that.

I didn't know if it was having him in my space, the only guy I'd ever let into this apartment. Or cooking him dinner and having him rave about it. Or having him tell me that he'd never spent the night at a woman's place so this would be a first. Or the way we'd connected during the first time we'd had sex in my bed. Or the second. Maybe even the third.

Whatever it was, I knew I was in trouble. Because this short-term fling had started to get to me a little.

I wanted to know what made Tanner King tick.

Realistically, nothing had changed. Once Remy was back on his feet and back at work, Tanner would leave. But I'd overheard him chatting to Makayla yesterday about opening another two clubs in Sydney, which meant he'd leave Le Miel but would still be in town.

After last night, short term had somehow morphed in my head into something possibly a little…longer.

I could lie to myself and say it was the sex. The phenomenal, stupendous, soul-drugging sex. But I'd given up lying to myself around the time I'd walked out on Bardley after finally admitting what a disaster I'd made of my life by kowtowing to everyone and lying to myself that I was okay with it.

So lying was out. Which meant I had to accept the fact I was in danger of falling for my sexy fling. No biggie. I'd have to suck it up, get my game face on whenever he was around and make sure he didn't see beneath my devil-may-care mask. Because I could care given half a chance and if there was one thing I'd learned during my brief time with Tanner, he wasn't the kind of guy to develop anything beyond a transient liking for.

I had clear-cut goals and I'd told him as such. No way would I let a little potential crush derail my plans.

I'd already given up so much in my life, had frittered away too many years being someone I wasn't for people who ultimately didn't give a crap about me. Emotional ties bred dependence and submissiveness and compliance, so no way would I allow myself to get involved with Tanner beyond the physical.

Moving forward, this time was for me. I intended to be selfish and goal-oriented, allowing nothing or nobody to distract me.

Tanner King in all his sexy, tattooed glory was one big distraction just waiting to happen.

So I wouldn't allow it.

After fifteen minutes of indulgent daydreaming, where I envisaged waking up to his magnificent body every morning, I'd slipped out of bed and got dressed as quietly as I could. He hadn't stirred, so I'd left him a breakfast tray next to the bed and a note. He wouldn't think it out of the ordinary that I'd started work at five, though he might take offence at being advised to slip out the back stairs if he didn't want to be spied doing the walk of shame.

In reality, I couldn't face Makayla's inevitable interrogation if she saw Tanner waltz in here wearing the same clothes as yesterday. For the simple fact I didn't know what I'd say.

Accepting I'd been idiot enough to be teetering on the brink of falling for him was one thing, admitting it to anyone else another. I could live with my secret.

I couldn't live with Makayla's endless banter if she discovered it.

For now, I needed to focus on my morning routine to get my head back in the game; and away from the sexy guy lying slumbering in my bed, waiting for a wake-up he'd never forget...

'Damn it,' I muttered as a glob of butter plopped onto the floor.

The intricate process of laminating dough to produce my signature Viennoiserie pastries required concentration and skill, neither of which I had this morning if my first effort was any indication.

So I started again. Wrapping a light dough around a layer of butter. Rolling it. Folding it. Rolling it again. Repeating the process over and over to produce a dough with many layers that would result in a puffy light texture that melted in the mouth after baking.

Remy said my almond croissants, *pain au lait* and *chouquettes* rivalled the best he'd tasted in France. I knew his excessive compliments were supposed to encourage me so I accepted them with aplomb, all the while wishing I could be half as good as my mentor.

So I toiled away every day, creating and tasting, buoyed by a lighter texture or a richer buttery flavour. Le Miel sold out on a daily basis so I had to be doing something right. And we often had orders for the almond croissants, which were solely my responsibility.

I'd come so far in a year I could hardly believe I was the same person. Thank goodness I'd had the guts to leave that subservient, pathetic people-pleaser who'd given up my dreams to live someone else's behind.

That was another thing sex with Tanner gave me:

empowerment. An intoxicating feeling of power that eradicated the shy girl I'd once been.

Performing my first blowjob might have been intimidating, but the way he'd reacted, the way he'd stared at me afterward...made me feel more powerful than I ever had. I might have been in a subservient position on my knees, intent on giving him pleasure, but the person I'd ended up pleasing was me.

I'd never felt so alive. So dominant. So in control. Heady stuff for the doormat I'd once been.

When I'd first proposed a fling to Tanner, I'd never anticipated that having my sensual side awakened would result in feeling this good. In making my body come alive, he'd also given me something I'd always craved: clout. Command over myself and my choices. The confidence to do what I wanted when I wanted, without regard for anyone else.

Something I'd secretly craved for years but never had the guts to do. Then again, it was easier with Tanner because we didn't have a strong emotional connection. I didn't feel the need to say yes to every little thing with him because our relationship focussed on the physical.

Which was exactly why I'd freaked out and come down here early this morning. Because no matter how many times I mentally recited that we were two consenting adults attracted to each other indulging in a short-term fling, after the way we'd connected last night and my desire to know more about him, I had a sneaking suspicion we could move past that.

And it terrified me.

The closer we got, would I be in danger of reverting to the meek, passive people-pleaser who always put others before herself? The woman who felt good about herself by making others feel good first? A guy like Tanner would hate that acquiescent docility and I'd hate myself for doing it.

Crap.

I concentrated on rolling and folding the dough over layers of butter, focussing on the routine to distract from my worrying thoughts, trying to relax. I liked the methodical approach to baking, the knowledge that following a clearly delineated process should result in an edible end product.

The routine calmed me, something I craved to deal with the riotous, out-of-control feelings ricocheting through me every time Tanner popped into my head.

He was there. A lot. Front and centre. Tanner shirtless and defiant in his private room at the club. Tanner stalking towards me in the storeroom. Tanner licking carbonara sauce off his lips. Tanner naked and sated, sprawled across my bed like he owned it.

Hell.

I opened the oven to slide the first batch of croissants in, the radiant heat not helping my fiery cheeks.

Baking might be comforting, but as a distraction from the hot male in my bed upstairs it left a lot to be desired.

Time to bring out the big guns.

I'd nail the elusive *croquembouche* today if it killed me.

Anything to divert me from the yearning to head back upstairs and have Tanner nail me.

CHAPTER SIXTEEN

Tanner

I HATED SNEAKING out of Abby's apartment like a fugitive, but I wasn't an idiot. She didn't want to face an
inquisition from her co-workers and that was exactly
what would've happened if I'd rocked into Le Miel
wearing the same clothes as yesterday.

Nothing got past Makayla. The woman had eyes in
the back of her head and I pitied the guy she set her
sights on. Bold ball-breakers weren't my type. I preferred quiet, reserved women who morphed into sex
kittens with the barest touch.

Women like Abby.

Leaving me breakfast had been just like her, a
thoughtful gesture reeking of unspoken sentiment.
Unfortunately, there'd been plenty of that going
around last night.

We'd barely spoken once we'd hit the bedroom.
Then again, words were superfluous when we both
suspected what was going on.

We'd potentially crossed the bonking buddies
threshold into some weird, nebulous territory neither
of us wanted to label. Not giving it credence suited

me just fine. Her too, considering she must've bolted out of bed at some ungodly hour.

So I scoffed my buttery soft chocolate croissant, drank my OJ and slunk down the back stairs, the words of her simple note imprinted on my brain.

Thanks for last night. Hope you enjoyed dinner.
Must do it again soon.
Back stairs quiet in the morning.
See you later.
Abby

Interestingly, no X. I thought all women liberally sprinkled kisses on their missives. Then again, I'd already established Abby wasn't like most women.

The 'must do it again soon' made me look forward to tonight in a way I shouldn't. I wasn't dating Abby. This wasn't a relationship. But dinner had been great and I'd like to return the favour. By taking her to my favourite restaurant in Sydney.

I'd never gone out with a foodie before, and considering her wealthy background, she'd probably dined at the finest restaurants this city had to offer. So I'd take her to my favourite hangout, a tiny Thai restaurant in the backstreets of Kings Cross, a place I'd give my left nut as a guarantee she'd never been to.

It wouldn't be a date. Just a friend returning the favour to another friend who'd cooked for me. Simple.

'You're full of shit,' I muttered at my reflection as I shaved, something I hadn't done for the last few days.

I didn't care about stubble as a rule, but Remy had always pulled me up on it ever since I'd been old enough to grow facial hair. Considering Remy would have enough to bust my balls about today, I didn't want to add another thing to the list.

The drive to the hospital took fifty minutes in peak-hour traffic, giving me ample time to come up with a plausible excuse as to why I'd shagged his protégé. By the time I'd parked and made it to the ward, I still hadn't come up with anything other than the truth.

Abby was hot and I had to have her.

Bet that would go down a treat with my brother.

I peeked into his room and saw Remy jabbing at the remote control, idly flicking channels, looking bored out of his brain. 'Hey, klutz, how are you feeling?'

'Better for seeing your ugly mug.' He turned off the TV and sat straighter in bed, wincing.

'Still in pain?'

'Only way these fools will give me the good stuff.' He made looping circles at his temple. 'That morphine makes me a little crazy, in a good way.'

I laughed and leaned down to give him a gentle man hug. 'You're perkier than last time, so that's a good sign.'

'Doc said I'm a model patient.' He screwed up his nose. 'Personally, I find it difficult to take the word of a punk wearing a white coat and stethoscope around his neck when he looks like he graduated from kinder last week.'

'Everyone looks young to you, you old fart.'

He pointed at his ankle and grimaced. 'Considering I'll have to use a walking stick once I'm on my feet, I may be living up to that insult.'

'You're only as old as the woman you feel,' I said, wondering what was Abby's age exactly.

'Sadly, I haven't been doing any "feeling" in a long time.'

When Remy pinned me with a speculative stare, I knew what was coming before he opened his mouth. 'What about you? Are you behaving?'

'I've got my hands full with the patisserie, if that's what you're asking.'

It wasn't and we both knew it, so I rushed on. 'Everything's going well. Customers still streaming in. Pastries sold out by the end of the day. Accounts balancing. Stocks replenished. Staff happy.'

Some happier than others, though Remy didn't need to know how I put a smile on Abby's face.

'You're shagging Abby,' Remy said, disappointment lacing every word as he shook his head. 'Man, I told you to keep your hands off her.'

'Since when have I ever listened to you?'

'You used to, once upon a time.' Remy eyeballed me, making me feel guiltier than I already did. 'You should try it again.'

I remembered the many times I'd listened to Remy, when he'd talked me down after yet another run-in with Dad, even if he hadn't known the reason behind my funk. When he'd persuaded me to stay rather than run away the time he'd found me hiding out in the back shed the week after Mum died. When he'd calmed me with words of wisdom on the day of Dad's funeral, painting a rosy future for us since he was over eighteen and could access the trust fund thoughtfully set up by Mum.

If it hadn't been for that money, and for Remy's calming influence, who knew where I might've ended up?

I owed him the truth. At least about Abby.

'I know I shouldn't have messed around with Abby. I'm not a complete doofus—'

'Could've fooled me.'

'But we both know where we stand so she won't get hurt.'

'You're a dickhead.' Remy snorted, his eyes narrowed in disapproval. 'You didn't see her the day she stumbled into Le Miel, disoriented and lost and sad. She hasn't told me much but her ex-husband must be a first-class bastard to do a number on a sweet girl like that and she's steered clear of men ever since.'

Remy jabbed a finger at me, a deep frown slashing his brows. 'So if she's let you anywhere near her, it means a hell of a lot more to her than it does to you. And you're going to fuck it up, just like you always do.'

A chill swept over me. Remy was my go-to guy. He always had my back. So what did he mean?

'Care to elaborate, bro?' My frigid tone did little to ease the sudden tension between us.

'You've never had a meaningful relationship with a woman. Whenever one of them gets close, you end it. That's what I meant.' Remy pressed his forehead, like he had a blinder of a headache building. 'Abby is different and if you hurt her because you couldn't keep it in your pants, I'm going to personally deck you.'

'Like to see you try,' I said, sounding meeker and suitably chastised.

Remy had never hit anyone in his life. I, on the other hand, had dealt out justice with my fists at high school on a regular basis. Bottled-up rage and a lousy self-esteem didn't mix, not when kids discovered which buttons to push to get me to explode.

'Not that I want to encourage this but, for what it's worth, when you walked in here you looked about a decade younger.' Remy stared at me, studying me with a slight tilt of his head. 'There's something different about you. You look less…stressed, or something.'

'Maybe working in a pastry shop rather than a club is good for me?'

He chuckled at my glib response. 'We both know that's not true.'

'Yeah, I know.' I reluctantly admitted, wanting to get the lowdown on Abby from Remy but knowing he'd be onto me if I pried too deeply. 'Abby's special.'

Remy's eyebrows shot up. 'Special to you?'

'I meant in general.' My clarification sounded lame and I continued. 'Hanging out with her makes me happy in a way I haven't been for a while.'

Remy's gaze turned speculative. 'You're sticking around for a few months, yeah?'

I nodded, trying not to acknowledge the leap of hope that the thought elicited. I'd already pondered the possibility of exploring more with Abby beyond our specified short-term fling, but she hadn't given any indication to wanting more and I sure as hell wouldn't stick my neck out.

I'd suffered enough rejection to last a lifetime.

'So you and Abby might be more than a passing fad?'

'Abby and I will sort out our own business, thanks very much.' I grinned at Remy's faux hurt. 'As for you, you old busybody, get better fast.'

Remy smiled but sadness lurked in his eyes, like he couldn't quite believe my flippant act.

'Both you and Abby mean a lot to me. Don't screw this up, okay?'

'I'll do my best not to.' I saluted. 'Anything else, captain?'

Remy hesitated, as if he wanted to say more, before he shook his head. 'Abby's important to me, professionally and personally, so take care of her.'

Sombreness was catchy as I nodded. 'I will.'

A promise I had every intention of keeping, if she let me.

CHAPTER SEVENTEEN

Abby

I DIDN'T HAVE time to wonder if Tanner had enjoyed the breakfast I'd left him or be grateful when he'd snuck out around six. Because at one minute past nine Makayla checked Le Miel's website and discovered we had a massive order for a ladies' function at Bondi. The kind of order that would send Remy into a tizz because of the possibility of repeat business. The kind of order to garner a week's profits in a day.

'How can we possibly do this?' Makayla printed out the order, her brow furrowed. 'It usually takes you and Remy working like maniacs to fulfil an order like this. Even then, it's touch and go.'

I should say no. It was lunacy even contemplating trying to fill this order. Besides, my first instinct to say yes sent a shiver of fear through me. I'd determinedly set aside my people-pleasing personality a year ago, had worked damn hard to ensure I learned to say no.

Then I glanced at the computer, saw Remy's face in the corner of our website's home page, and my fear faded.

Agreeing to tackle a big challenge for the man who'd given me a break when I needed it most wasn't being servile. It was a way of helping out a friend who'd helped me, a way of giving back. I owed Remy and I knew without a doubt he'd rather I tackled this massive job than wimp out.

'What time do they need it by?'

Makayla stared at me like I'd lost my mind even contemplating this. 'Delivery at two thirty for afternoon tea at three.'

'Shit,' I muttered, scanning the list and mentally prioritising. 'We can supply the mini-croissants from the lot I baked this morning and put the "Sold Out" sign out front. Then I can make the strawberry tarts, the apple turnovers, the *pains au chocolat* and the beignets—'

'You're crazy. You'll never get all that done.' Makayla gnawed at her bottom lip and rustled the paper at me. 'Seriously. We're going to have to outsource—'

'Remy never does that. He hates putting his name to products he didn't make.'

'I know, but what can we do? We're screwed.'

I heard a footfall behind me. 'What's the problem, ladies?'

My heart leapt in recognition, and something akin to happiness, as I turned to Tanner. 'A massive order just came in. Big profits. And I can't do it without Remy.'

He stared at me, brows furrowed, eyes clouded with an unfathomable emotion I could almost label as fear, before he blinked and swiped a hand across his face. When he lowered his hand, determination accentuated the lines around his mouth, like he'd come to a decision and wouldn't let anything or anyone derail him.

'I can help,' he said, rolling up his shirtsleeves, making me salivate a little at a glimpse of those striking tattoos. 'What do you need me to do?'

I appreciated the offer but I still couldn't shake the feeling he didn't want to be here. Saddened by the thought it could be because of me and our newfound intimacy last night.

'Unless you're a secret pastry chef, there's no chance in hell we can do this—'

'I can cook.' He rubbed his hands together. 'Let's get this done.'

'I admire your tenacity but with all due respect being able to cook a steak on a barbecue and being able to create pastries worthy of the Le Miel name are worlds apart.'

One of his eyebrows quirked. 'You're doubting my skills?'

He made *skills* sound like I doubted his prowess out of the kitchen, and Makayla stifled a chuckle behind me.

'This isn't a joke, Tanner. This is Remy's reputation on the line if we can't deliver—'

'Then stop wasting time and let's get cracking.' He strode into the kitchen, leaving me gaping after him— and unable to resist staring at his mighty fine ass.

'Something tells me you two won't need any ovens in there, you generate that much heat between you,' Makayla said, her gaze speculative as she stared after Tanner too. 'Look, we've got nothing to lose. Let him help. Get as much done as you can and if you can't do it all I'm sure we can substitute the strawberry tartlets with lemon from the front store, and swap *pain au chocolat* for *pain au lait* from the massive batch you made early this morning at some ungodly hour.'

Makayla's eyes narrowed. 'Though why you'd be down here baking when you could be kneading some prime male is beyond me.'

I tended to agree with her.

'No time to chat,' I said, and Makayla laughed at my brusqueness. 'Get in touch with the contact person on that order and ask if they're okay with us substituting some of the items.'

'Yes, boss.' Makayla saluted, then shooed me towards the kitchen. 'Now go cook with that delicious man.'

'This is a recipe for disaster,' I muttered, dragging my feet.

I liked Tanner. I liked that he was ready, willing and able to pitch in at a time like this. I didn't like having to babysit him while I tried to concentrate on producing quality pastries in the fastest time possible.

Trudging into the kitchen, I was surprised to see him with apron on, hairnet and cap in place, with sugar, butter, flour and eggs in the correct quantities lined up in front of him on Remy's workspace.

'What are you doing?'

'Making croissants,' he said, like it was the most obvious thing in the world that a nightclub owner could create Viennoiserie pastries. But he still hadn't lost the haunted look, like being in the kitchen terrified him, and it worried me. 'Remy taught me when we were teens, so I've got it covered.'

He waved at my workstation. 'You get started on the rest.'

Stunned, I stared at him as he sectioned the butter and measured out the precise amount of flour.

'Babe, I know you love perving on me, but you're wasting time.' He dusted his hands with flour and blew me a kiss, creating a tiny flour cloud in the air. 'We've got an order to fill.'

Speechless, I headed to my workstation, methodically working through the pastries I needed to make while trying not to sneak peeks at Tanner, who appeared to be an expert in laminating dough and creating the perfect croissant.

I couldn't believe it as he produced symmetrical and equal-sized croissants, filling two trays of fifty each.

'One hundred enough?' he asked, sliding the trays into the oven and setting the timer.

'Yeah,' I said, sounding a little awestruck. 'Is there anything you can't do?'

'Climb the Harbour Bridge.' He wrinkled his nose. 'Afraid of heights.'

'Well, lucky for me you're not afraid of getting elbow deep in flour,' I said, putting the finishing touches on the strawberry tartlets. 'I can't believe you made those croissants.'

'I'm a man of many talents,' he said, puffing out his chest in mock bravado. 'As I'm sure you can attest to.' He came up behind me and placed a kiss on the nape of my neck, sending a shiver of delight through me. 'You're pretty hot when you're concentrating.'

He pressed against me, showing me exactly how hot he found me, and I groaned, rubbing my butt against him.

'Later,' he growled, nipping at my neck, my earlobe, before seeking out my mouth for a quick peck. 'I've already pissed off Remy enough this morning. Let's not add to his distress by mucking up this order.'

'You've already been to see him?'

He came around the front of my workbench and I glimpsed worry in his eyes. 'Yeah, visiting hours start at eight, I was there at seven.'

'You told him about us?'

He nodded, the grooves bracketing his mouth deepening. 'It went as I expected. Him warning me off you, me reassuring him I wouldn't hurt you.'

'Then what's the problem?'

He hesitated before shaking his head. 'No problem. My brother's a worrywart, always has been. He thinks this may get more complicated than either of us anticipated.'

I didn't want to tell Tanner I agreed with Remy.

Labelling Tanner the tattooed rebel as prime sex-toy material to purge my past had been fine at the start. But after having dinner with him last night, having him spend the night and now, watching him create incredible pastries like he did it every day of the week, I knew we were in serious danger of moving past a casual fling and into some nebulous, murky area I dared not label for making things *complicated*.

'But right now, our only complication is who's going to make the *pains au chocolat*, and if mine's better than yours, what are you going to do about it?'

I chuckled at his cockiness and jabbed a finger towards his workspace. 'You get started on them, I'll make the beignets.'

'I love it when you're bossy,' he said, with a wink. 'In and out of the bedroom.'

Heat crept into my cheeks and I waved him away. 'We've got three hours to get the rest of this order done. Let's do it.'

'And later tonight, we'll *do it* for real,' he said, his voice low and husky, making me yearn for him to bend me over and fill me in the way only he could.

'Work first,' I said, clearing my throat, my hands shaking a little as I reached for the flour.

'Speaking of tonight, I'd like to take you out to dinner.' He threw it out there, casual as you like, like asking me out on a date was an everyday occurrence. 'Nothing fancy, but my favourite Thai place will soon become yours if you enjoy spicy Asian fusion.'

'Sounds great, thanks.'

How I managed to sound offhand, I'd never know, while inside I did whirls and sidekicks.

'Pick you up at seven thirty?'

'Okay.'

We didn't talk much after that, as we focussed on creating pastries worthy of the Le Miel name. But I was super aware of him working alongside me, the big, bad, baker boy, making delicate pastries with ease, making me crave him something fierce.

Was there anything sexier than a man who knew his way around a kitchen? For me, no. I liked a guy confident with a bowl and spatula, a guy who could combine sugar, eggs and flour and create magic, a guy like Tanner.

I liked Tanner. A lot. Today had solidified my feelings into one crazy, scary ball of longing deep inside.

The way he'd pitched in, the way he'd made a potentially stressful situation fun, the way he'd taken charge, all incredibly attractive.

But it was more than how he looked or how he behaved. Tanner was a good guy, despite doing his best to appear otherwise with the tats and the glower. He attracted me on some subliminal level I had no hope of analysing or explaining.

I wanted Tanner. Perhaps for longer than our short-term fling. Which begged the question: What happened to me at the end of our arrangement when he didn't want the same?

I'd had the guts to walk away from my marriage and had been all set to walk away from Tanner with just as much nonchalance. Easy in theory, much harder in practice.

I'd never wanted to make this difficult. I'd wanted a casual, fun fling to take the edge off my otherwise routine life. I'd wanted to experience steamy sex with a hot guy. But now that we'd potentially moved past that…I had to admit to being worried.

I'd come so far in a year. I didn't want a relationship where I could potentially revert to the meek, compliant woman who'd do anything to keep the peace and her partner happy.

That kind of commitment scared me. I had my goals. If I had Tanner in my life for longer than a few weeks, would I lose sight of them? I didn't want to find out.

Remy had every right to be concerned.

Tanner and I were one big complication waiting to happen.

And there wasn't one damn thing I could do about it.

CHAPTER EIGHTEEN

Tanner

'I DON'T BELIEVE THIS.' I glared at the sign hanging in the window of my favourite Thai restaurant, announcing they were closed for renovations. 'I didn't even think to book because it's one of those walk-in places that rarely requires a reservation.'

'Don't worry about it.' Abby laid a hand on my arm. 'We can eat anywhere.'

True, but I'd wanted to show her a place that meant something to me, to see how she acted in the surroundings. Not a test, as such, just a way of convincing myself that while we connected physically we could never be anything long term.

Looked like the cosmos had punished me for being underhanded and I'd have to resort to Plan B. If I had one.

'Honestly, I'm not fussed where we eat.' She patted my forearm and removed her hand. 'It's been a long day, so I'd be happy with fast food and an early night.'

'You just want to get me naked as soon as humanly possible,' I said, grinning when she blushed. 'You're so predictable.'

'Am not,' she said, with a defiant tilt of her head. Her nonchalant act would've worked too, if I hadn't glimpsed the naughty gleam in her eyes. 'I am hungry, but if you want to grab something and head back to my place…'

Best invitation I'd heard all day but this date was about proving a point and that was exactly what I'd do. Our strong sexual connection wasn't conducive to showing her how different we were outside the bedroom and how we could never be anything more than bonking buddies.

'How about fish and chips on Manly beach?'

If my subtle change of subject surprised her, she didn't show it. Instead, she nodded. 'It's a long way from the Cross to Manly by car.'

'We'll take the ferry.'

Her eyes lit up. 'Would you believe I've lived in Sydney my whole life and never been on the Manly ferry?'

'Never?'

She glanced away, her shoulders slumping a little. 'I got chauffeured everywhere. By Dad, our chauffeur and later Bardley's driver.'

'*Bardley*. I still think it's such a bullshit name,' I snarled, hating the stab of jealousy at her casual use of her ex's name.

'Totally.' She laughed and slipped her hand into mine. 'I've never eaten fish and chips on the beach either, so I'm in.'

Wouldn't her family have a fit if they knew their little princess was being taken on a no-frills date involving simple food and a ferry? It made me wonder, did she miss her old life at all?

She might hate her ex but it had to be tough living a life of luxury, then leaving it all behind. Considering how hard we'd worked today filling that urgent order, she must do that all the time with Remy. Throw in the small apartment, and it had to be a big comedown from her previous life. I admired her all the more.

'Do you miss your old life?'

She stiffened as we strolled back to the car. 'Where did that come from?'

'Curiosity.' I opened the car door for her and waited until she sat before closing it and getting in the driver side. 'Bit of a comedown, switching from chauffeurs to ferries.'

She took an eternity to answer, as if formulating an acceptable answer. 'I miss my family. And some of my friends. But that lifestyle was never important to me.'

That was where we differed. Every luxury I could afford now was testament to how far I'd come. How far I'd proved Father wrong.

Not that I took my wealth for granted or flaunted it, but I revelled in my hard-earned success. And thanked the old bastard every day for spurring me on to become the man he never thought I could be.

'So you're not in touch with anyone from your old life?'

We stopped at a traffic light and I shot her a glance. Her lips were compressed and her arms folded, protecting herself from…what? Memories? Sadness? Me?

'No.'

A short, sharp response that clearly meant she didn't want to talk, so I remained silent until we reached Circular Quay, bought tickets and boarded the ferry.

But I couldn't let it go. Gaining an insight into her past would make it easier for me when this thing between us ended. I liked Abby. I didn't want to hurt her. Knowing what made her tick beyond the superficial would ensure I could let her down gently. 'Have you ever thought about getting in touch with your family?'

I expected her to shoot me down again with a death glare. Instead, she stared at the Opera House, lost in thought.

'Yeah, I think about getting in touch with Mum. I miss her.' She dragged her gaze away from the white sails and focussed on me. 'You'll think I'm an idiot, but I even drove past a day spa we used to go to together the other day, hoping for a glimpse of her.'

'You miss her. That's not stupid.' I slung an arm over her shoulder and cradled her close. 'I miss Remy when I'm overseas. It's normal. Family has a way of getting under our skin.'

Though not always in a good way. Dad had been testament to that.

'I can't believe she hasn't reached out after a year, you know?' She rested a hand on my thigh, a comfortable, intimate gesture that secretly thrilled me.

She trusted me. Trusted me enough to talk about her past. But was I worthy of that trust?

'A whole year without so much as a phone call.' She shook her head. 'What kind of a mother does that?'

I didn't have a clue, considering I had nothing but good memories of mine and our happy times in the kitchen. But I had to offer some comfort, otherwise this date was heading south fast.

'I'm guessing your father rules the roost, so maybe

she's doing the best she can, trying to keep the peace in her marriage and not piss him off?'

Respect shimmered in her eyes as she gazed up at me from beneath long lashes. 'Dad is the boss and what he says goes, but she wouldn't have to tell him.'

'If she's anything like you, I can't see her sneaking behind his back. You're far too principled for that and she probably is too.'

'Stop sounding so logical,' she said, her admonishment tempered with a smile. 'Anyway, enough of my depressing family.' Her smile faded and she squirmed a little, appearing uncomfortable. 'I don't know much about your family beyond the fact your parents died when you were young.'

I stiffened, my thigh flexing involuntarily beneath her palm, and she stroked my leg, offering comfort. If she only knew…it would take a lifetime of placating to ease the pain any thought of my parents elicited.

'Is that all Remy told you?'

She nodded. 'Said your mum died when he was fifteen, your dad when he was twenty.' Pity darkened her eyes. 'That means you would've been ten when you lost your mum…must've been tough.'

'You have no idea.'

Mum had been my champion, my rock, my buffer. She kept Dad away from me, sensing his hatred even though he never did anything overt towards me in front of her.

And I blamed the old prick every day for ultimately driving her to her death. Because of me.

'Tell me about her.' Abby spoke softly, her tone laced with gentle persuasion, like discovering more about my family background would somehow give her a handle on me.

Yeah, like that would happen.

But I'd prompted her to discuss her family—the least I could do was give her a snapshot of mine.

'Dad didn't have much time for me, so Mum and I were close. She taught me how to cook. How to choose a good mango. How to core apples for a classic turnover until my fingers ached…' Bittersweet happiness filled me at the memories. 'She was French. Very elegant. Very classy. Wore make-up and perfume every day, even when dropping me off at kinder. Everyone idolised her.'

Except Dad. I'd never known the real reason their marriage soured until I'd heard the hurtful accusations he'd flung at her the day she'd died. But he'd definitely been in the minority, because everyone loved Mum.

'She sounds wonderful,' Abby offered with a smile. 'Was that why you looked a little freaked out when you helped fill that massive order? Did being in the kitchen again dredge up memories of her for you?'

Surprised by her insight, I nodded. 'She was wonderful. And every time I set foot in a kitchen, even at home, I feel it right here.' I thumped a fist over my heart, wishing the simple action could dislodge the permanent ache there whenever I thought of Mum and how much I missed her.

Before I could think up something to change the subject, Abby continued. 'What about your dad?'

'He was a prick.' The words tumbled from my lips before I could stop them and if she heard the venom behind them, she didn't say.

Her hand resumed stroking my thigh. 'How so?'

'He hated my guts.'

Her lips parted in surprise. 'But you were a child. How could a father hate his own child?'

I couldn't tell her the truth. Not when I'd never told anyone, including Remy. So I settled for a watered-down version.

'Their marriage hit a rocky patch. I was the spitting image of Mum. Guess that made me dislikeable.'

Her nose wrinkled in distaste. 'I'm not in the habit of slandering people I've never met but your dad sounds like a real piece of work.'

'Understatement of the year,' I muttered, annoyed that her quick defence meant so much.

This date had been about proving our differences, not growing closer because of shared confidences. I needed to get back on track, fast.

'Anyway, Remy is the only family I have and he more than makes up for the past.'

I could see the turmoil in her eyes, like she wanted to prod further. Instead, she said, 'Tell me how many women you've taken on ferry dates before.'

Surprised and pleased at her change of subject, I grinned. 'As of today, only one.'

She made a cute scoffing sound.

'You don't believe me?'

'I believe you've been a bad boy since you hit your teens and I imagine you've had a string of girlfriends.' She poked me in the chest. 'So don't try to deny it.'

'I'm not denying anything.' I held up my hands, like I had nothing to hide. 'I just haven't taken any of them on a ferry.'

'Lucky me,' she said, batting her eyelashes with exaggerated coquettishness.

'I'm the lucky one,' I murmured, wondering what she'd do if she could see half the thoughts whirling through my head. 'I know what this fling is about for you. A way to move forward. A way to ditch your past once and for all.'

I squeezed her shoulders. 'I'm lucky you picked me to do it.'

An odd expression flitted across her face. Regret? Anger? Hope? But it disappeared faster than I could analyse it.

She snuggled into me as the ferry chugged its way across the water. We made desultory small talk, about the Harbour Bridge, Luna Park and the mega cruise ships sailing through the Heads. Nonsensical stuff that I didn't give a crap about, but safe conversation. Safe from the possibility of emotions or feelings or deeper truths.

Like how much I wanted her to enjoy this simple date and possibly see the real me. The me beneath the tattoos and smart-ass attitude. The me who could fall for a girl like her given half a chance.

But there was a world of difference between us and if there was one thing I'd learned from Father, it was that I couldn't be a relationship kind of guy.

I couldn't be selfless, not after spending too many years feeling worthless. When he'd died, I'd vowed to use every ounce of bitterness and resentment and hurt to concentrate on being a guy worthy of success. A guy worthy of recognition. A guy worthy of every good thing in life.

Being involved with a woman like Abby would ensure I wouldn't be number one any more. I wouldn't only care about myself and not give a damn about her. I'd need to let her in, let her see the deepest part of me where a smidgeon of that scared, worthless kid still resided.

I wasn't prepared to do that.

'We're here,' I said unnecessarily, as the ferry docked and passengers started disembarking.

'Good, I'm starving.'

She held my hand like it was the most natural thing in the world as we placed our order at the outdoor fish 'n' chip pop-up café, squeezing it when we confessed a mutual hankering for grilled barramundi and extra chicken salt on our chips.

If only it were that simple, that similar taste in food could be the foundation of something more permanent between us.

Because that was the kicker amid all my ruminations. While I didn't want a full-blown relationship that required giving too much of my private self, I wouldn't mind continuing our arrangement for however long I was in Sydney.

But Abby had clearly stipulated a short-term fling at the start. Besides, she deserved more. I'd seen the way she'd started looking at me, and while I liked it I couldn't shake the feeling that Abby developing real feelings for me would only end in heartache.

I carried the paper-wrapped parcel as we strolled towards the beach, in time to watch the sun dip behind the horizon in a blaze of mauve and indigo.

'Wow,' she said, slipping her hand out of mine to bound to the sand. 'I know you're a master of many talents, but organising a sunset like that is too much even for you.'

'Anything for you,' I murmured under my breath, grateful she couldn't hear me.

Sure, I'd wanted her to enjoy this date, to see the simple pleasures I liked, but I'd also wanted to prove a point to myself. That we were nothing alike and she'd probably prefer a Michelin-starred dining experience to this.

But seeing her obvious joy when she unwrapped the paper, snagged a piece of fish in one hand and stuffed hot, salty chips into her mouth with the other made me want her more.

'This is divine,' she mumbled, her mouth half-full, and I laughed. The kind of laugh I hadn't done in a long time. A laugh filled with genuine happiness of being in this moment with this woman.

'What's so funny?' She wiped her mouth with a tissue she'd fished from her handbag. 'Let me guess, I'm not like your previous stick-insect model girlfriends who only ate salad.'

'A fact I'm eternally grateful for.' I offered her more chips, pleased when she took another handful. 'What's with you and my old girlfriends? Jealous?'

'Pfft.' She crammed the chips into her mouth to refrain from answering and I grinned.

'It's okay to like me, you know. Thousands have in the past.'

Her eyebrows shot heavenward. 'Thousands? Eww, that's just nasty.'

I laughed, enjoying the banter we traded. 'Well, I may be exaggerating a little.'

'Phew.' She swiped at her brow. 'I can deal with hundreds. Thousands? Not so much.'

'Interesting that you see me as some shallow playboy.' I leaned my hands back, propped on outstretched arms on the sand. 'Truth is, I'm not a relationship kind of guy, but that doesn't mean I sleep with every woman that walks.'

'Just the ones that drop their panties at your feet,' she deadpanned, her eyes alight with mischief.

I loved seeing her like this: playful and light-hearted.

'The only panties I'm interested in dropping these days are yours.' I deliberately stared at her breasts before sweeping lower to linger where those sensible cotton panties would be.

'Stop that,' she hissed, wriggling on the sand a little.

'Why, am I making you horny?'

Her gaze flew to mine, her lips parted in shock.

'It's okay to admit it, you know.' I crooked a finger at her. 'I'll let you in on a secret. I'm half-hard every time I'm around you, and most times when I'm not, just thinking about you.'

'Oh,' she said, so softly I barely heard it as her gaze dropped to my groin.

Predictably, I stiffened, my hard-on straining against the fly of my jeans. Damn, I should never have started this game.

'Told you we should've grabbed takeout and gone back to my place.' She almost purred, her tone soft and seductive. 'Now we have a long ride back on the water.'

'Fuck that ferry,' I muttered, not pleased that our sweet date had morphed to sexy in an instant, even less pleased that I had to be in blue balls hell for an entire ferry ride back to the city.

'It'll be much more pleasurable to f-fuck me,' she said, turning crimson at saying the F word.

'Stop,' I groaned. 'Why do you choose now to start talking dirty?'

She leapt to her feet and dusted sand off her butt, her grin smug. 'Maybe we should grab a taxi rather than wait for the ferry?'

'Maybe you're right,' I said, bundling up our rubbish and stuffing it in the trash on our way back to the road. 'Better buckle up, babe, because I'm going to tell the driver to break the land speed record.'

A coy smile played about her mouth as she stood on tiptoe and pressed a kiss to my lips. 'Thanks for dinner. It was the best date I've ever had.'

Speechless, I flagged down a taxi and bundled her in, almost tumbling in after her in my haste to get her alone. Where I could show her with actions rather than words exactly how much I'd enjoyed our date too.

CHAPTER NINETEEN

Abby

I USUALLY LOOKED forward to my day at TAFE once a week, a day to take a break from the manic pace of Le Miel and absorb the theory behind creating pastries.

I loved the lectures, the note taking, the practical sessions. The sight of my notebooks covered in scrawl. The sharing of recipes with fellow students. The questions fired at the visiting chefs.

I loved it all. But today I was distracted, seriously distracted. And I blamed a tall, tattooed nightclub owner with a penchant for pastry and me.

Last night had been incredible. A laid-back evening filled with laughs and loving. Making love, that was. I'd never be foolish enough to confuse it with any other type of love.

During our beachside date, Tanner had been more relaxed than I'd ever seen him. He had a softer side to him that was just as appealing as the harder edges. I liked seeing his different facets, like peeling back the layers of an onion and discovering more intricacies beneath.

He'd come back to my place after our beachside

picnic and we hadn't left the bed for hours, before falling asleep in each other's arms. When he'd left at five this morning, he'd seemed different. Almost reluctant to depart. More tender somehow.

It had freaked me out a little. I couldn't let Tanner derail my plans. I'd already given up so much of myself in the past and now that my divorce had come through and I was finally free, I needed to move forward. To do what was right for me.

As much as we burned up the sheets and the many ways I craved him, having anything beyond short term with Tanner would be a recipe for disaster.

I knew what would happen. I'd end up getting emotionally invested, wanting to do whatever it took to keep my man happy and end up resenting him, ensuring one of us would walk away. And I'd be catapulted back to twelve months ago, picking up the pieces of my life while struggling to heal, while cursing my lack of a backbone.

After coming so far, I couldn't do that to myself. I wouldn't.

Determined to forget the possible complications with Tanner and focus on today's lectures, I hoisted my backpack higher and headed for the imposing wrought-iron front gates, mentally reciting the day's timetable.

Deep in thought, I stumbled over a crack in the footpath.

And almost slammed into my mother.

'Hello, Abigail.' She helped me straighten, her expression half fearful, half expectant, as she released me. 'How are you?'

'Fine,' I responded by rote, stunned to see her here, torn between wanting to hug her and throttle her.

I'd missed her so much. Had she missed me at all?

A tsunami of mixed emotions swamped me: anger, sadness, hope, regret. A potent combination that made my hands shake and I clenched and unclenched them a few times to get a grip.

I'd envisaged the first meeting with Mum or Dad so many times late at night, when I'd been cradling a Chardonnay and trying to ignore the insistent little voice in my head that recited how much my parents didn't give a damn. In those thoughts, I'd imagined Mum hugging me, squeezing me so tight like she'd never let go. Maybe even Dad apologising and begging for forgiveness.

But there'd been no hug from Mum. No sign that this was anything but an orchestrated encounter for who knew what purpose.

'You look tired,' she said, studying my face, her intense scrutiny not bothering me like it once had.

How many times had I heard her berate me?

'Abigail, you need to use more moisturiser on your frown lines.'

'Abigail, sunscreen is an important part of your beauty regimen. You don't want to wrinkle before fifty, do you?'

'Abigail, those dark circles under your eyes could do with a thicker concealer.'

'Abigail, that shade of coral lipstick makes you look too pale. Try a vivid pink.'

I'd tolerated her beauty advice because it was her thing, like I accepted her criticisms of everything from my wardrobe to my haircut. She was my mother and it'd been easier to acquiesce than cause dissension and ultimately get the silent treatment. I'd hated when she'd ignored me.

Ironic, as she'd given me the ultimate silent treatment over the last twelve months.

If she'd been trying to teach me a lesson, it hadn't worked. The only thing I'd learned was that I should've escaped my parents' shadows and started living my own life a long time ago. And that I couldn't trust those closest to me, despite how much I loved them.

Hoping the emotion clogging my throat wouldn't make my voice shaky, I said, 'I'm busy, so maybe we can catch up another time?'

She wrinkled her nose, considering she couldn't wrinkle her perfectly smooth Botoxed brow. 'You don't have to be busy, you know. Working at that pastry place, going to school here once a week.' She waved her hand at the TAFE, then in front of her nose, like the place stank. 'It's beneath you.'

Ice trickled through my veins. This definitely wasn't how I'd envisaged our first meeting after a year. There were no kind words, no professions of missing me, no hugs.

Instead, it was the same old. Mum telling me what I should and shouldn't be doing.

I crossed my arms across my middle, desperate to quell the hollow ache that her indifference elicited. 'How do you know where I work?'

Not that I particularly cared what the answer was. They'd obviously wanted to keep an eye on me, to ensure I hadn't entered prostitution or anything similarly nefarious that would bring disrepute on the precious Prendigast name.

'You know your father likes to keep tabs on everyone.' She patted my arm, the briefest touch that conveyed nothing but condescension. 'We care—'

'Cut the crap, Mum. If you cared, you would've tried to contact me over the last year. To at least pretend you loved me more than keeping up appearances. To show you were worried about me rather than your reputation.' My voice had risen and several students glanced our way, so I blew out a calming breath. 'Look, arguing is pointless. I need to get to class so—'

'Come home,' she said, her expression dour as she stared at me with distaste. Heaven forbid a Prendigast showed real emotion. 'It's not too late. You can salvage your marriage to that poor boy Bardley, resume the life you should have, repair our name—'

'You don't get it,' I said, mentally counting to ten to quell the rising anger making my hands shake. 'I'm happy. I'm leading the life I want, not the life you want me to.'

'Don't be ridiculous,' she snapped, bitterness twisting her mouth. 'You're behaving like a child. You've had your fun for a year, time to grow up.'

I stared at the woman who'd given birth to me, with her powder-blue designer suit, perfectly streaked blond hair, immaculate make-up and a handbag that would pay my rent for two years.

My mother.

Who wouldn't know the meaning of the word if it jumped up and bit her on her surgically tightened ass.

A few moments ago, I'd been filled with hope that she'd sought me out to offer a smidgeon of understanding, that she'd finally understood my rationale for walking away from my old life and wanted to embrace me with acceptance.

What a crock.

Bone-deep disappointment shook me to my core. I loved my parents; all I expected was to be loved in return. But this wasn't love. And if I was completely honest with myself, had they ever loved me at all?

Love wasn't controlling and dominant and angry. Love didn't expect me to acquiesce and bow down to the heavy weight of expectations. Love didn't leave me alone for twelve long months, without making the slightest overture to heal a rift.

The ache in my stomach spread into my chest, reaching outward until I could hardly breathe. I needed to escape, to get away from her obvious disapproval.

There was no love here, only judgement, and I couldn't tolerate it a moment longer.

'Bye, Mum. Don't contact me again.'

How I managed to get the words out without breaking down I'd never know, but I did, sounding surprisingly calm when I was a screaming mess inside. A seething mass of emotion that threatened to spurt out of my eyes in a torrent.

My mother drew herself up, squaring her shoulders for a fight that would never come. Because I was done. 'Abigail! Don't you dare walk away from me.'

So I did just that, without looking back.

CHAPTER TWENTY

Tanner

'WHAT THE HELL did you tell those doctors to bully them into discharging me early?' Remy propped on his elbow crutches, grinning at me with newfound respect the following Tuesday. 'On second thoughts, I don't give a flying fig what you said. I'm just rapt to be going home.'

'And back to work as long as you keep off that ankle and just supervise,' I added, playing the solicitous brother to the end and feeling like a fraud because of it.

Getting Remy discharged from hospital hadn't been an altruistic act on my part. I needed him back at Le Miel.

So I could leave.

Continuing to work alongside Abby after this morning was untenable.

For the first time ever, when I'd woken next to a woman after another incredible night of sex, I hadn't wanted to leave.

I'd wanted to stay. In her bed. In her apartment. In her life.

Ensuring I had to leave pronto.

I wasn't a forever kind of guy. I'd end up driving away anyone who got too close. I'd had that drummed into me from a young age, the reason why I'd made such a big effort with Remy to prove Dad's prediction wrong. At least he'd died knowing I was loyal to my brother. I hoped he choked on the knowledge when he looked up at me from hell every single day.

'I can't thank you enough for holding down the fort while I've been in hospital.' Remy cleared his throat as I picked up his bag. 'You've been amazing.'

'Save the mushy crap for someone who cares,' I said, sounding just as gruff as we exited his room and made our way slowly up the corridor towards the exit. 'Do you want me to drop you home or at Le Miel?'

'The patisserie, of course.' He waved one crutch around. 'The ankle feels fine in the boot and these things are okay for my ribs, so all good.'

I'm glad it was all good for one of us. Me? Not so much. I had to extricate myself from the thing with Abby and every time I thought about ending it I felt sick in my guts.

I wanted her in my life.

I'd end up pushing her out of my life.

Which meant the kind thing, the honest thing, would be to finish it now before either of us got invested.

Too late for me. I was already in way too deep and flailing like a drowning guy. Desperate to grab onto the nearest buoy, which happened to be my brother returning to work.

'You wait here and I'll go get the car—'

'What's wrong?' Remy stopped me by stabbing

my foot with a crutch. 'Did something bad happen between you and Abby?'

'We're fine,' I said, summoning a latent acting skill I'd honed to great effect as a kid, knowing it would fool Remy. He'd never seen through my fake bravado, from the first time I tried to hide my tears at age eight when Dad yelled at me for looking like 'that useless French slut who trapped me into marrying her' to the many times since Mum died and his systemic verbal abuse made me feel worthless and useless like nothing else could.

At the time, I'd resented Remy for not being around, for not seeing enough, for not doing anything. I'd hated him deep down for being caught up in his apprenticeship and his schooling and his dreams of running a patisserie one day.

But as Dad's emotional torture had escalated, I'd been glad Remy hadn't been around to notice. Dad had ruined my life; I didn't want him tainting Remy's as well. Remy was a good guy. He looked after me when he could. I was lucky to have him as a brother.

After Dad died, Remy had broached the topic of my obvious animosity towards our father once. I'd ended up throwing Dad's prized beer stein against the wall, smashing it to smithereens and laughing hysterically. Remy had put my tantrum down to grief and the teenage hormones of a fifteen-year-old running wild but, thankfully, he'd never brought up the subject since.

So I summoned those infamous acting skills now to force a nonchalant grin. 'It's been great working alongside her.'

Remy's eyes narrowed, pinning me with a glare

that said he didn't believe my bullshit, not this time. 'I'm not talking about work and you know it.'

'We've had fun.' I shrugged, feigning indifference I didn't feel, wishing that damn ache in my chest would quit sooner rather than later. 'We're good.'

'Had, as in past tense?' Judgement laced his tone. 'So you're over?'

Feeling like a prick for lying to my brother yet again, I nodded. 'You know me. I'm not built to last.'

'You're full of crap.' Remy snorted, shook his head. 'She's a great girl. You're staying in town. Why not see where this can go?'

I knew exactly where this would go. Down the toilet.

'I'll get the car,' I said, stalking away.

My usual MO and I'd stick to it.

I just hoped Abby would understand.

CHAPTER TWENTY-ONE

Abby

ENJOYING A RARE lull after the morning rush, I sipped on a soy latte in the kitchen, mentally sorting the baking tasks for this afternoon.

However, every time I got to item three on my to-do list, thoughts of Tanner would intrude, ensuring all my concentration focussed on him and him alone.

It was no use denying it any longer. I'd fallen for him.

And I'd almost made the fatal mistake of telling him this morning.

It had been so comfortable, so easy, waking up next to him, making idle chatter about our day ahead. There'd been a moment, a drawn-out fraught moment, where I'd thought he was on the same page as me. He'd stared into my eyes, taken my hand and opened his mouth to say something.

I'd held my breath, waiting for him to say he didn't want this to end. That he wanted to explore a relationship. That he wanted me for more than a few weeks.

Instead, he'd raised my hand to his lips, brushed a

kiss across the back of it, before rolling on top of me and consuming me whole.

He did it very well, distracting me with his body, bringing me to life in a way I'd never dreamed possible. So I'd given over to the pleasure, biding my time.

I'd tell him. Soon. And hope to God he wouldn't run.

He'd left my apartment early, citing an appointment, but something had been off. Almost like he'd closed down after our monumental wake-up sex.

Maybe he'd sensed my impending revelation? Maybe he'd been tired from the few hours' sleep we'd got yet again? Whatever the reason, he'd be back to help out any second and I'd keep things strictly professional in the kitchen before asking him to a cosy dinner tonight.

Where I'd lay it all on the line.

The back door creaked open and I straightened, my hand drifting unconsciously to my hair and tucking stray strands into the net holding it off my face.

Tanner strode through the door, his expression unreadable as he held it wide open and waited.

'Hey, what's... Remy?' I squealed as my boss hobbled into the kitchen, a grin as wide as the Harbour Bridge splitting his face. 'What are you doing here?'

I flew across the kitchen to give him a tender hug, surprised but thrilled to see him.

'Doc discharged me early because I'm healing well. So I'm back on deck.' He mock frowned and glared around the kitchen. 'Lucky for you, everything seems to be in order.'

I whacked him on the arm. 'Tanner and I have not

only held down the fort, we've filled major orders and turned a handy profit.'

'Remind me to give you a raise.' Remy's eyes twinkled with warmth. 'Seriously, kid, you've done an amazing job and I can't be more grateful.' He half turned to Tanner, who hadn't moved from the door. 'To both of you.'

'He's back to the mushy stuff,' Tanner said, rolling his eyes, and I chuckled. 'Let's get him set up on a stool or chair or something, so he can start issuing orders and be a general bossy pain in the ass.'

The bell from the front of the patisserie tinkled, indicating a customer. 'I'll have to get that. Makayla popped out and Shaun called in sick today.'

Remy waved me away. 'Go. Tanner will get me set up.'

'Great to have you back.' I gave him another impulsive hug before bounding down the corridor towards the front of the patisserie.

And pulled up short when I saw who the customer was.

'What are you doing here?' I half closed the door between the front and the kitchen, not wanting Remy or Tanner to hear me send my mother on her way. 'You need to leave. Now.'

To my mother's credit, she didn't flinch from my icy order. 'I've come to apologise.'

'For what? Twenty-two years of not believing in me? For wanting me to be your clone? For shoving your expectations on me, then treating me like crap with the silent treatment if I didn't give in immediately? For not supporting me through a loveless marriage? For having the gall to ask me to come back and live in that charade, all for the sake of your precious ego?'

Sadness downturned her crimson-lipsticked mouth and she shook her head. 'I deserve that.'

'And a whole lot more. But this isn't the time or place. I'm working.'

'I know.' She glanced around, approval in her brusque nod. 'I used to love walking past this place, but I never dared enter for fear of putting on two pounds just by looking.'

Mum had been past here but never come in? Maybe she did possess a soul after all and had wanted to keep an eye on me? Then again, if she really cared, she would've wanted to talk, to hug, to forgive. Instead, she'd waited twelve long months before confronting me at uni, demanding I kowtow yet again.

I hated the flare of hope deep inside when I'd first spied her here today. Because after all I'd been through with my parents, I should know better. She hadn't succeeded in convincing me to bow to the Prendigast way first time around; today would be round two.

She walked to the front display cabinet and trailed her fingers over the glass. 'Everything looks so delectable. Those tiny macarons. The croissants. The tarts. I'm drooling.'

'I made all that,' I said, squaring my shoulders, expecting a put-down or a backhanded compliment at best. 'It's what I love doing.'

'You're lucky, following your dream.' She cleared her throat and turned back to face me. 'That's why I'm here, actually. To help you.'

'I don't need your help.'

I didn't need anything from her, not after the way

she'd abandoned me when I needed her most, then chastised me for it last week, imploring me to come back and 'all would be forgiven'.

As if.

Mum sighed and smoothed an imaginary wrinkle from the hem of her jacket. 'I know there's nothing I can say to make up for staying away this past year. Or the way I treated you when I ambushed you outside TAFE.' She waved her hand towards the display cabinets. 'But I'm hoping that my actions will speak louder than any trite apology I could come up with.'

Curiosity tempered my resentment. 'You're talking in riddles.'

'I came here to extend an olive branch.' Mum took a deep breath and blew it out. 'If being a pastry chef is your dream, I want to help you achieve it. So I'm willing to fund your very own patisserie. Wherever you want. I'll pay the lease for as long as you want. Or I'll buy the building.'

While I struggled to comprehend the words pouring out of my mother's mouth, she continued. 'No strings attached. I don't expect you to forgive me. But I'd like to be a part of your life again. To make up for lost time…' She trailed off, her voice soft. 'I think I was jealous of you, for having the guts to do something on your own, for not always conforming, like I do.'

She shook her head, her blond bob swinging lightly across her shoulders in blow-dried perfection. 'I've been telling myself for years that I'm happy with your father calling the shots, that I lead a full, happy life. But in the end, what do I really have to show for it all, apart from a designer wardrobe, a sports car and killer hair?'

I couldn't help but smile. Mum had always been vain about her sleek blond bob.

'For what it's worth, I'm sorry, Abigail. For everything.' She took a tentative step towards me, unsure of my reaction.

I hesitated, wanting to broach the gap between us, wanting the past to fade away, wanting so much but afraid to be let down yet again.

'Abigail, please…'

I couldn't ignore the wavering plea in her voice or the generous offer. So I walked towards her and into her embrace.

Tears burned my eyes and I let them fall, inhaling my mum's familiar rose fragrance, savouring the comfort of her hug. I'd needed this, needed her. Guess it was better late than never.

When we eased apart, her eyes were bloodshot and she blinked rapidly, as if to stave off further tears.

'So what do you say? Fancy being your own boss?'

Her offer had blown me away but I needed to couch my rejection in terms she'd understand.

'I appreciate the offer, Mum, I really do. But I want to keep learning from Remy and complete my apprenticeship here.'

When her mouth drooped in disappointment, I added, 'But after that, who knows? I'd love to run my own patisserie.'

'That's great.' She held my hands and squeezed. 'I'm sorry it's taken me this long to say it, but I'm so proud of you.'

'Thanks, Mum, it means a lot, coming from you.'

She held me at arm's length, her smile genuine. 'Your father's a stubborn old goat, but I'm hoping he'll come around too.'

'Don't hold your breath.'

My dry response earned a chuckle. 'If he doesn't, I don't want that to affect our relationship.'

'Seriously?' My incredulity was audible. 'Did you ever wonder why I was such a mouthless, subservient yes-girl?'

Mum blushed, sadness clouding her eyes, but if we were to have any chance at a real relationship moving forward, I had to be completely honest.

'I'm sorry, Mum, but I copied you. Dad ruled the roost. Whatever he says goes. And if you didn't agree, he'd treat you with frosty silence. Me too.' I shook my head, let down by the person I'd been, but pleased to have come so far. 'So I started modelling you and it soon became easier to acquiesce with everything than cause problems.'

Tears shimmered in her eyes. 'Your childhood wasn't that bad, was it? We loved you. We gave you everything—'

'Life isn't about having everything. It's about being true to yourself.' I gestured around the patisserie. 'I feel more alive here than I ever did.'

I saw Mum's crestfallen expression but it didn't stop me. She had to know how bad things had been so we could move forward.

'I'm not blaming you entirely, Mum, but growing up in a household where it was easier agreeing to everything ensured I didn't say no when I should've, like agreeing to marry Bardley.'

Obstinacy twisted her mouth. 'But you grew up

together. He's a nice boy and you had so much in common—'

'I never loved him and he turned out to be a controlling, verbally abusive prick.'

She didn't flinch at my swearing. Instead, she appeared to wilt before my eyes, her usual proud posture defeated.

'I don't know what to say...'

'I didn't tell you all this to make you feel bad.' I patted her arm. 'I just wanted you to know why I've fought so hard to become independent and to follow my own dreams, not live yours.'

She nodded, her eyes clear with clarity at last. 'You've been honest with me so I'll return the favour. I don't expect your father to come around. He's still livid at your "antics".' She made air quote marks. 'But I'll do my best to make him see reason.'

'Thanks, Mum.'

This time, I leaned in to give her a brief hug. To her credit, she hadn't baulked at my revelations or tottered out of here on her designer heels. Maybe there was some hope for us to re-establish a mother-daughter relationship. A real one, free of domination and subservience and lies.

'I'll be in touch but in the meantime if you need anything you call me, okay?'

'Okay.'

She kissed my cheek, cast me a final confused glance like she couldn't figure me out, before sailing out of the patisserie, leaving a cloud of rose-scented air in her wake.

There'd been no mention of a specific catch-up. No mention of coming home for a meal. But for now, it was enough. I knew my mum and her coming here to offer me my own patisserie had been a big gesture on her part. Huge.

It was a start.

Later, I'd mull our exchange at length. For now, I had a stack of beignets to bake and loads of news to catch Remy up on.

Starting with how his brother had stolen my heart without trying and I had no idea what to do about it.

CHAPTER TWENTY-TWO

Tanner

THE MOMENT I heard Abby's mother offer her a patisserie I should've eased away from the door and headed
back to the kitchen.

When we'd initially heard Abby's raised voice,
Remy had sent me to the front to investigate but I'd
stopped short when I'd peeked around the half-closed
door and spied Abby in a standoff with a woman.

I had to admit curiosity had got the better of me
when I'd heard Abby call the immaculately dressed,
perfectly coiffed older blonde 'Mum'.

So this was the dragon that'd abandoned her daughter for an entire year. She didn't look so bad. Then
again, most people had thought my father looked like
a frigging saint and he'd had the black soul of a devil.

I'd been so proud of Abby, standing up to her
mother. But it sounded like this wasn't the first time
they'd met up. I'd heard something about Abby being
ambushed outside TAFE.

Which meant she'd lied to me. She'd said her
parents hadn't been in contact over the last twelve

months, yet she'd obviously seen her mother. Why would she keep that secret?

If I'd needed proof that she only saw me as short-term fling material, this was it. Obviously I wasn't to be privy to her family dealings, not when we had a clear expiration date.

A date I'd deliberately brought forward today.

I hovered at the door like a goddamn sneak, long enough to witness their happy reunion. Abby had forgiven her mum. She'd accept the patisserie. She'd be welcomed back into the family fold. Who knew? She might even find some other rich prick from her social circle to hook up with.

Wasn't any of my concern. That ache in my chest had to be heartburn from downing three steaming espressos at the hospital.

In a way, Abby's decision made things easier. I'd had a gutful of being second best growing up. This time, I wouldn't stick around to be anyone's second choice. Never again.

Leaving them hugging and in tears, I backed away from the door. Time to hit the road.

When I strode into the kitchen, Remy was flicking through one of Abby's notebooks, covered in her flowing scrawl and overflowing with recipes cut from newspapers and magazines.

I'd teased her about the many notebooks lying around her apartment. She'd said it was her thing, to let it go, but I'd loved watching her sit in her favourite armchair, idly flicking those pages, worrying her bottom lip with her teeth, as a small satisfied smile played about her mouth.

She loved her job and it showed. She'd be a great

pastry chef, good enough to give Remy a run for his money. Good luck to her. Pity I wouldn't be around to see her success.

'What happened out there?' Remy flipped the book shut and laid it on the bench. 'Abby sounded upset.'

'It's her mother.'

Remy gaped at me, like I'd announced a visit from the Queen. 'She's here?'

I nodded and jerked a thumb over my shoulder at the front of the patisserie. 'They've made up.'

'Good for her.' The concern clouding Remy's eyes didn't dissipate instantly. 'That family has a lot to make up for, abandoning Abby like that.'

'I agree.' I made a grand show of looking at my watch. 'Now that you're back, bro, I've got a ton of work to catch up on. So take it easy. I'm outta here.'

I should've known Remy wouldn't let me leave so easily. 'But you're coming back, right?'

I could've made up some bullshit story. But this was Remy. I couldn't do it. Not to him.

'No.'

A short, sharp refusal that hung in the air like a stinky pall. Heavy and oppressive. Stifling anyone unlucky enough to be near it.

'You're leaving?' Disgust curled Remy's upper lip. I didn't blame him. I disgusted myself too.

'I'm staying in Sydney but I won't be around here to help any more.' I thrust my hands in my pockets, alarmed to find them shaking a tad. This was it. The break from Le Miel. And Abby. 'You've got it covered. I'll check in on you at home and if you need me for anything, just call—'

'You're running scared. Again.' Remy spat the

words out, staccato and stabbing. 'Let me guess. You're not even going to say goodbye to Abby.'

Feeling like a low-life bastard, I shrugged. 'I'll call her—'

'You'll *call* her? How fucking magnanimous.' Remy sneered, his loathing nothing on what I felt myself. 'I can't believe I thought you'd changed, that this time might be different.'

I shouldn't ask. I really shouldn't, but I found the question spilling from my lips. 'Different, how?'

'You've looked lighter, happier, than I've ever seen you.' Some of Remy's anger faded as his face relaxed into an expression bordering on antipathy. 'I knew it was Abby. She was good for you. And judging by the way she lit up earlier when you walked in the door, I'd say the feeling is mutual. But you're going to screw it up again. Run like you usually do. Pretend that you're a big tough guy not affected by your past, when in fact it consumes you.'

'You're talking out your ass,' I snapped, clamping down on the flicker of fear Remy's accusations elicited. 'And keep your psychobabble bullshit to yourself.'

'No. This time you listen.'

I'd never heard Remy like this, his tone low and lethal. Ice cold. Chilling.

'Dad did a number on you. I get it. For some unknown reason he hated you, and I'm sorry I wasn't around enough to figure it out earlier. But he's gone. He can't hurt you any more, so why are you letting him?'

I gaped at Remy in open-mouthed shock. I'd never spoken to him about Dad. Had gone out of my way to put on a brave face the few times Remy was home to eat dinner with us. Had deliberately pretended I was fine while he chased his dream and I lived at home with a monster that blamed me for every bad thing that had happened in his life.

I could deny it now. But what was the point? Besides, it might do me good to offload some of the bottled-up crap, considering I was screwing up with Abby because of it.

'How did you know?'

Remy slumped, aging before my eyes. 'The day before Dad died I came home early. Heard you two arguing. Heard some of the stuff he said to you…' Remy's voice broke and he cleared his throat several times before he could continue. 'I hated myself for not knowing, for not being more aware. I was going to talk to Dad about it, and to you, but then he had that heart attack the next day and it seemed pointless dredging it all up when you seemed so relieved.'

'Best fucking day of my life.'

Sadly, it could never trounce the worst. The day I'd overheard my parents arguing, the day I'd learned why Dad hated me, the day Mum had been so upset she'd driven off in anger, swerved off the road and hit a tree, dying on impact.

Remy's eyes glittered with realisation. 'Did he ever hit you?'

I shook my head. 'Not punches, just the good old-fashioned wooden spoon on my ass, but the rest was worse…' Then it all came bubbling out, like a lanced boil, filled with putridity. 'He grabbed me a few times, rattled the living daylights out of me while yelling the usual abusive crap. About how I looked like Mum and that was a constant reminder of how he'd made the worst decision of his life to marry her.'

My chest heaved with the effort of subduing sobs. 'But he didn't stop there. Because tolerating his crap and me asking what was behind his hatred was like uncorking a genie bottle; unfortunately for me, vitriol appeared and I sure as hell didn't get any wishes.'

I wanted to tell Remy all of it but I couldn't. If he looked shattered by my partial revelations, the rest would undo him completely and I couldn't be responsible for that.

A derisive chuckle, devoid of amusement, exploded from my mouth. 'When you were around, he behaved normally. When you weren't, he heaped praise on you and acted like I didn't exist. When he wasn't accusing me for being as useless as Mum, that is. I pretended like the constant put-downs meant nothing. That I was impervious to whatever he said. But even now, I still think I'm not good enough. That people can see through me to the unworthiness beneath...' I sounded broken, frail, and it mortified me.

I'd hidden everything from Remy, had not wanted to worry the brother I idolised. Remy had been my rock, the one constant in a crappy childhood. For him to now know how badly I was fucked up... I should've felt better, finally confessing, but it made everything one hundred times worse.

'Fuck, I'm so sorry, I had no idea...' Remy's voice hitched and his face crumpled as he swiped a hand across his eyes. 'Why didn't you tell me—?'

'Not worth both of us having a shit upbringing.'

My eyes burned but I'd be damned if I shed one tear over that old bastard. My brother staring at me like

I'd stabbed him in the heart, that was another matter entirely. I wanted to blubber like a baby the longer he gawked at me with pity visible in his tear-filled eyes.

'You really feel unworthy still?'

A question I didn't want to answer because it sounded pathetic articulated out loud. At my core was that bitter young boy, filled with resentment and anger and hatred, but helpless to do anything about it.

When I didn't respond, Remy slumped further, appearing to sink in on himself. 'Shit, I'm so sorry, Tanner. But look how far you've come.' Remy gestured at the door, his eyes glistening with tears I'd caused. Me. It tore me apart all over again. 'Out there is an amazing woman who I'm pretty sure is head over heels for you and you're walking away because—'

'Because she'll ultimately walk away from me. Her mother just offered Abby her own patisserie,' I hissed through gritted teeth, the futility of all this washing over me like an icy wave. 'Don't you get it? I'll never be good enough for someone like her.'

A lone tear trickled down Remy's cheek. 'You are the best—'

'Thanks, bro, but it is what it is.'

I had to get out of here before I lost it completely. Or worse, Abby came back in.

'Say bye to Abby for me.'

I didn't wait around to hear Remy's response as I bolted out the door.

CHAPTER TWENTY-THREE

Abby

I DABBED AT the moisture under my eyes with my pinkies, not wanting Remy and Tanner to interrogate me about the reason behind the tears when I re-entered the kitchen.

I couldn't believe it. Mum making a grand gesture. Seeking forgiveness. Re-establishing contact without trying to direct my life. Despite blaming them for so much, I'd missed my family and after our last confrontation had given up all hope of ever being part of the Prendigasts. But if Mum had made an overture, I hoped Dad would follow and, eventually, we'd be a family again.

Not like before, with me afraid to voice an opinion or following their lead for everything, but in a mature way where we respected each other.

I could live in hope.

I paused at the kitchen door, breathed in and out a few times, before fixing a smile on my face and striding in. Only to find Remy slumped at a bench, head in hands, looking like he'd received devastating news.

Tanner was nowhere to be seen.

Foreboding strummed my spine as I approached him. 'Hey, everything okay?'

When he raised his head and his agonised, blood-shot gaze met mine, I knew it wasn't. In fact, something bad had happened in the few minutes I'd been out front, and I rubbed my bare arms against the sudden chill sweeping over me.

'Where's Tanner?'

He shook his head, his expression so morose I wanted to hug him. 'Gone.'

'Did you two fight?'

'No.' He swore, something he never did, and I pulled up a stool alongside him. 'There's no easy way to say this, but he's not coming back.'

Confused, I leaned closer. 'What do you mean? Not coming back to help here? That was inevitable, but—'

'He's gone, Abby.' He spoke softly, barely above a whisper. 'And he asked me to say goodbye to you.'

It took a second for understanding to dawn, and when it did I slumped against the bench too, filled with horror and disappointment and eventually numbness. An icy, debilitating chill that spread from my chest out, making my arms and legs tingle then shake.

It did little to anaesthetise the pain twisting my gut, making me want to vomit.

'What happened? I was only gone a few minutes.'

I couldn't comprehend it. This morning in bed he looked like he cared way beyond casual. Now he'd walked away from me without even saying goodbye? It didn't make sense. Sadly, I had a feeling nothing Remy said would clarify my confusion.

'Tanner's in a funk and when he's overwhelmed,

he runs.' Remy pinched the bridge of his nose. 'It's what he's always done.'

'Am I the cause of that funk?'

Remy had the decency to meet my gaze when he nodded. 'I think so. I've never seen him so happy. It's why I thought this time would be different.'

A stab of jealousy pierced my sadness. 'So he's done this before with other women?'

'No, he's never let other women get this close.' A deep frown slashed Remy's brow. 'You're a first, which is why I thought he'd make a stand and fight.'

'I don't understand. He's in a funk because he's happy?'

Remy nodded, sorrow turning down his mouth. 'He thinks he's not good enough for you.'

'What?' Incredulous, I pressed my fingers to my temples to try and make sense of all this. 'He's successful, rich and hot. Why would he think he's not good enough?'

A slow-burning anger overtook my indignation. 'And I'm not going anywhere, so why would he think I'd leave?'

Remy faced me, his expression morose. 'Has he mentioned our parents?'

I nodded. 'Yeah. Sounds like he idolised your mum but your dad was awful.'

'Okay, so you know some of it...' Remy shook his head. 'It's not my place to tell you everything I just learned, but let me say this. Tanner has been through a hell of a lot and he's hurting...' He shrugged, a simple gesture filled with helplessness. 'It really messed with his head. Explains why as soon as he inherited his trust fund he rebelled, determined to do his own thing and prove himself to the world.'

A picture formed in my head that broke my heart. A boy losing his parents too young and becoming emotionally stunted because of it. A child with an inherent lack of trust for anyone other than the brother who stood by him through everything. Now that boy had become a man who shunned intimacy because of that lack of trust.

But I'd never given him any indication that I would hurt him.

Other than the clearly articulated short-term nature of our liaison.

Hell. I'd basically told him at the start that I was one of a long line of people in his life who wouldn't stick around. No wonder he'd bolted when he'd thought we might be getting serious.

I muttered a curse under my breath. 'What can I do?'

Remy patted my arm. 'Honestly? Nothing. I know from experience that once Tanner makes up his mind, nothing or no one can change it.'

He glanced away, his furtive look not filling me with confidence. 'He thinks that once you'll open your own patisserie, you'll be absorbed back into your old life and you won't want him cramping your style.'

'What the...?' I shook my head, confused again. 'But I'm not opening my own patisserie. I mean, maybe one day, but I'm happy here.'

Remy's expression lightened as he eyeballed me. 'But he overheard your mum's offer and thought you'd accepted?'

'He misconstrued.' I made crazy circles at my temple. 'That's what happens when you listen at keyholes.'

He managed a wan smile at my dry response. 'So you're staying?'

'For as long as you'll have me.' I leaned over and gave him an impulsive hug. 'You saved me when I needed it most. I'd never betray you.'

'It's not a betrayal to embrace your family again,' he said when we'd sat back. 'I saw how gutted you were when they abandoned you.'

'Honestly? I'm trying to give Mum the benefit of the doubt with her generous offer, but a part of me can't help but feel she's trying to buy my forgiveness?'

He nodded, his brow furrowed in thought. 'You could be right, considering the length of time she's taken to approach you. But she's your mother. Take it from someone who lost my mum far too early and who'd give anything to have more time with her. Don't waste time analysing her motivation. Just give it a chance.'

I reached over and squeezed his hand. 'Thanks. You're a good friend.'

'Anytime.' His smile faded as the frown slashing his brows returned. 'As for Tanner, I think you need to give him time. Space. Let him brood. Sulk. Whatever.'

He held up his hand and crossed his fingers. 'And hopefully this time, he won't screw up the best thing to ever happen to him.'

I valued Remy's advice. But as someone who'd walked away from a relationship without looking back, I hoped Tanner wouldn't do the same.

CHAPTER TWENTY-FOUR

Tanner

'YOU'RE IN A foul mood.' Hudson strolled into my office and perched on the edge of my desk. 'Woman troubles?'

'Fuck off,' I snarled, not wanting to talk about Abby. Now or ever.

'Nice.' Hudson tapped at the screen of his cell and turned it towards me. 'What do you think of this?'

Work I could do. Work would keep me focussed and driven. Work I could understand. Unlike the tumultuous feelings eating at me from the inside out, tainting every waking moment and most sleeping ones too.

It had been three days since I'd walked out of Le Miel. Seventy-two long hours where I'd fought every instinct to contact Abby. To explain. To apologise. To do something to ease the pain she must be feeling.

Because if she felt half of what I was feeling, she'd be in frigging agony.

I squinted at the screen. 'A live show?'

Hudson nodded. 'Lots of the Vegas clubs are doing

them these days. Hosting special live events to draw in the crowds.'

'We're not known for being a live venue.'

'Which is why this is so innovative.' He brandished the cell at me again and I swatted it away. 'What's happened to the guy always ready to take a risk?'

I'd taken a risk with letting Abby into my life and look how that had turned out. Risks were for suckers.

'Do a proposal. Set out figures for me. Then email me and I'll take a look.'

'That's the spirit.' Hudson gave me a thumbs up. 'Now how about we hit the town tonight? Boys' night out. Involving copious amounts of alcohol and luscious babes. What do you say?'

The thought of being near another woman right now set my teeth on edge. Crazy, because Abby and I were over. I owed her nothing. But it was too soon.

'Thanks for the offer, but I'll be working late tonight.'

Hudson stood and huffed out a breath. 'Look, at the risk of getting my teeth punched out, you've been locked away in here for three days straight. You snap at anyone who ventures close. The staff are afraid of you. And I'm sick of you treating me like an enemy rather than a friend.'

He jabbed a finger at me. 'So do whatever it takes to lighten the fuck up, okay? Confront what's got you so riled. Get it out of your system. Deal with it.'

The only thing that would lighten my mood was to see Abby again and that wasn't going to happen. Not in this lifetime.

'Thanks for the pep talk, mate,' I drawled, and

pointed at the door. 'Now get the hell out and leave me alone.'

'Dickhead,' he muttered, shaking his head as he strode towards the door, where he paused. 'For what it's worth, I liked you better when you were dating that Abby chick. She made you happy.'

I made a growling noise and stood, my fingers clenching into fists.

Hudson held up his hands in surrender. 'Just saying,' before he closed the door on his way out.

Abby had made me happy but that was over.

The faster I got my head around it, the better.

CHAPTER TWENTY-FIVE

Abby

'WHAT DO YOU THINK?'

I glared at Makayla as my back twanged for the umpteenth time. 'I think Pilates is for pretzels.'

'It's your first class. You'll get the hang of it after a few more.' Makayla interlinked her fingers and stretched overhead. 'It's brilliant for flexibility and core strength.'

'I'll take your word for it.' Wincing, I managed to stand. 'In the meantime, I've got a hot bath with my name all over it.'

'Fancy going out tonight?'

It had become Makayla's standard invitation over the last three days. Ever since Tanner had walked out of my life and I'd let him.

'Thanks, but I'd rather chill.' I rolled my shoulders, hoping they didn't spasm. I had a big croissant order to fill tomorrow.

'A night out might do you good.' Makayla slung a towel around her shoulders and mopped her face. 'Get him out of your system.'

Nice in theory. Sadly, I had a feeling it would take a lot of practice to get Tanner out of my system.

'You're a good friend. But I'm okay, honest.'

A total lie, but I'd managed not to shed a tear yet, and I aimed to keep it that way. Easier to keep busy at work, then watch mindless sitcom reruns at night and fall into bed exhausted. I had a feeling if Makayla started asking questions about why things ended with Tanner, delved too far beneath my fragile surface, I'd crack. Once that happened, everything I'd been keeping locked away tight might spill out and that would be disastrous.

'You don't have to lie to me.' Makayla slumped onto a bench lining the mirrored wall of the exercise studio and patted the spot next to her. 'I can see how much you're hurting all over your face.'

I grimaced as I sat next to her. So much for my poker face. 'That obvious?'

'I've been there. It sucks.' She shrugged. 'Did he give you a reason why he split?'

'Uh...we haven't spoken.'

Her eyebrows shot up. 'What do you mean?'

'When Remy got back, he left, and we haven't spoken since.'

Makayla stared at me in confusion. 'You haven't called him to ask what's going on?'

'Nope.'

'Why the hell not?'

'Dignity. Pride. Nonchalance. Take your pick.'

'You're nuts.' Makayla elbowed me. 'It's been three days and you haven't wanted to see him? To talk to him?'

I knew exactly how long it had been since I'd last

seen Tanner, beyond that fleeting glimpse when he'd brought Remy in. The morning I'd left him sexy and sleepy in my bed. The morning he'd held my hand, stared into my eyes and opened his mouth to say something, possibly momentous, before he'd chickened out.

I had too. I could've nudged him, given him another opportunity. Instead, I'd bolted for the shower and waited until he'd left before coming out of the bathroom. If I'd known that would be the last time I'd see him, would I have done things differently? Probably not. I was lily-livered that way.

I hadn't known what had scared me more that morning: the possibility of Tanner saying he wanted a long-term relationship or me saying hell yeah.

'Remy and I had a chat. He advised I give Tanner some time to brood.'

'Wrong.' Makayla made a buzzing noise. 'Guys like him will retreat into their man cave, mull over the situation, invent reasons to suit their argument, then never call again.'

A sliver of doubt pierced my previous calm. I'd assumed Remy knew best. He'd given me insight into Tanner's state of mind and I understood his need to think things over.

But what if Remy's advice had missed the mark in this instance? What if I'd played this all wrong, giving Tanner too much time?

It made me wonder. What would've happened if I'd approached my family after I'd left? Would they have been more amenable to hearing my side of the story once the initial shock of my defection wore off? Would we have had some semblance of a relationship rather than this weird standoff that had finally been broken by my mother?

I'd been so busy playing the victim this last year, too busy blaming them, to realise that I could've made the first move.

Establishing my independence was one thing. But I'd let the hurt of being judged and then abandoned by them taint my view.

Once I'd got past Mum's initial rants about ruining the Prendigast name and bringing shame on the family, I could've reached out. Could've explained how downtrodden I'd felt my entire life. How Bardley had made my life hell.

I could've revealed how observing Mum kowtow to Dad on every single issue ensured I did too. That I hated his quick temper when he lashed out for the slightest disagreement. That it was easier to say yes to whatever they wanted than tolerate the emotional shutdown and icy silences that followed the few times I'd tried to take a stand. That being a people-pleaser became so ingrained that it had taken me a year to finally feel like I had a backbone.

Instead, I hadn't told them the truth about how I'd felt. I'd given them time and space too. Just like I was doing with Tanner.

Hell. Had I made a monumental mistake?

'Listen, honey, you need to talk to him. Three days is too long to leave a guy to his own devices.' Makayla swivelled to face me, tugging on the end of her ponytail, a gesture I'd come to realise meant she was worried about something. 'Who knows what bullshit excuses he'll come up with for you two not to get together?'

She patted my arm, her smile warm. 'And trust me, you two belong together.'

I liked her confidence. Pity I didn't share it.

'Why? Because we're both dysfunctional when it comes to relationships?'

'Because I've seen the way you two are around each other.' She bumped me gently with her shoulder. 'It's like no one else's in the room. You've only got eyes for each other.'

'You read too many romance novels,' I said, knowing exactly what she meant, because that was how I felt when Tanner was around.

Like all he could see was me.

Heady stuff for a girl who'd always been second best to everyone else. Tanner made me feel wanted and cherished and important in a way I never had. And that was during our supposed fling.

What would it feel like to have a real relationship with a guy like that?

Considering how I might have mucked this up, I'd probably never know.

'Go see him.' Makayla nudged me again, more forceful this time. 'Besides, you fought for your independence from your family. You fought to follow your dream to bake. Why wouldn't you fight for love?'

My instinctive response, 'I don't love him', died on my lips.

I hadn't loved Bardley and I'd felt nothing but sadness I'd put up with so much for so long when I'd walked away from him.

I hadn't seen Tanner for three days and I felt like my insides had been ripped out, put through a blender and stuffed back into me in disarray.

If that was love, did I really want any part of it?

Then again, Makayla was right. I'd fought hard to get where I was. I'd fought family expectations, social constraints and a possessive husband to gain freedom.

Tanner had become an important part of my life, no matter how hard I tried to dismiss him as bad-boy fling material to purge my past.

If I didn't put up some semblance of a fight, I'd end up regretting it, and I'd had a lifetime of living with regret already.

Makayla must've seen something in my face, because she smiled. 'Go home. Clean up. Then knock him dead.'

'Thanks.' I hugged her, emotion clogging my throat.

She wriggled out of my embrace and swatted me away. 'And don't forget, I'll expect details tomorrow.'

'If I make it into work.' I winked, knowing I'd never let Remy down but hoping I wouldn't get much sleep once Tanner and I made up.

'Go get him, girlfriend.' Makayla gave me a thumbs-up sign of encouragement as I tried to quell an aviary's worth of butterflies slam dancing against my rib cage.

I would confront Tanner.

Ensure he wouldn't shut me down.

I had a lot to say and I'd make sure he listened.

CHAPTER TWENTY-SIX

Tanner

FOR TWO HOURS after Hudson had left my office I tried to focus on work. But my concentration was shot and I ended up reading the same spreadsheets ten times, numerous applications for a cocktail waitress that blurred into one, and staring unseeing at the architect's plans for an upcoming venture.

Shit.

I stood and stretched, working out the kinks in my back, feeling like I'd wasted an entire afternoon and had nothing to show for it.

Grunting in frustration, I picked up my keys and cell. Maybe a workout at Jim's would help. But as I drove out from the underground car park, a sparring session lost its appeal. The mood I was in I was liable to knock someone's head off and that wouldn't be good for anybody.

I pulled up at a traffic light, hating the indecisiveness that plagued me. Usually, when I made decisions I stuck to them. But my head was a whirl of dark thoughts, mostly centred on how I'd screwed up yet again.

As the light changed to green, something Hudson had said reared up like a grizzly demanding to be heard.

'Confront what's got you so riled. Get it out of your system. Deal with it.'

Easier said than done. I'd love to confront the prick that'd done such a number on me that I still heard his derisive voice in my head sometimes. Berating me. Castigating me. Putting me down.

A crazy thought pierced my self-pity. There was a way I could confront him. Do something I hadn't tried before to put the past behind me. It wouldn't come close to coming clean face-to-face, but it would be a gesture I could've tried a long time ago.

Feeling like a fool, I headed for the small cemetery on the outskirts of Surrey Hills.

I'd only been to the place once, on the day of Dad's funeral. I hadn't wanted to go. Remy had made me, citing it would look bad if I didn't show and might raise red flags with Social Services that he had no control of me and therefore would be a lousy guardian.

The thought of losing the one person who meant anything to me was enough to scare me into an ill-fitting suit and into the neat cemetery where a handful of mourners had gathered.

It didn't surprise me that hardly anyone turned up for his funeral. He hadn't had many friends. People rarely came to visit. He didn't go out. Maybe if he'd socialised more, he wouldn't have focussed all his attention on me; and not in a good way.

Considering his hatred of me stemmed from Mum, he must've made her life hell too but she'd hidden it from us kids. We'd never gone on outings as a family and he'd kept long hours, coming home late from the building site to sit on the couch in front of the TV, more interested in the news than Remy and me.

We'd done our homework in the kitchen, with Mum pottering around, content to listen to the recount of our days. She'd ply us with snacks and make us laugh, her impulsive hugs growing more frequent the more Dad withdrew.

On the rare Sundays he was home, I had a vague recollection of being shunted into the backyard with Remy to play while they talked in the house. Though Mum wouldn't last long inside and she'd soon join us on the back lawn, where we'd play tag or cricket.

Until that fateful day when I'd heard raised voices and my first instinct was to protect Mum. She never shouted, so for her voice to reach me in the furthest corner of the backyard meant things were bad. Remy had been at a friend's birthday party, leaving me to decide whether I should keep weeding or check if Mum was okay.

I chose the latter. And what I overheard explained so much.

I'd hidden behind the back door as the argument escalated, frozen in shock, wishing I were bigger so I could punch my father and knock him out for saying such hateful things.

Tears had burned my eyes but I'd refused to cry. I needed to be strong. For Mum.

She'd spied me when she'd rushed out the back door, her eyes red-rimmed and swollen, her mouth trembling. She'd gathered me close, squished me in the way she always did, and I'd felt her shaking. She'd said she had to go for a drive and she'd bring me back my favourite humbug lollies.

She never came back.

Her car had veered off the road and into a tree less than two kilometres from our house. The police hadn't been able to explain the cause of the accident but I knew. She'd been so distraught by the disgusting, vile accusations hurled by my father, she hadn't been concentrating on the road.

Thankfully, brake marks and the pattern of skid showed she'd tried to avoid the tree, because I couldn't have handled the fact she'd been hurting so badly she would've abandoned me to that monster.

That day when she got in her car, I remember being scared, left alone with Dad after what I'd overheard.

Little did I know that hour would turn into five miserable years where I'd tolerated whatever the old bastard dished out, wishing every single day that he'd been the one to die instead of Mum.

Surprised to find my eyes moist with unshed tears, I pulled into a parking spot and composed myself before heading into the cemetery.

He didn't have a fancy gravestone. Remy had opted for a small plaque that simply had his name, date of birth and death, and RIP. Rest in peace my ass. I hoped he was squirming in hell, hopping around to avoid the flames.

I stood over the plaque, glaring at it, resisting the urge to kick it. Why should he rest in peace when I'd had nothing close to peace because of him?

'You were a piece of work,' I said, thrusting my hands in my pockets, rocking on the balls of my feet as if spoiling for a fight. 'You were a mean, spiteful bastard that made my life hell. Which is where you're at now and I hope you're burning.'

Stupid, talking to a piece of stone, but it somehow felt cathartic. So I continued.

'Remember that time you locked me in the cellar because I didn't eat my broccoli? Well, the joke was on you, because the first thing I did when you let me out was go dip your toothbrush in the toilet.'

I grinned at the memory of my first rebellious act at ten, a few months after Mum died.

'Then there was that time you made yourself a stack of strawberry pancakes and gave me half a bowl of dried apricots? Well, let's just say there wasn't just sugar in your tea every night, because some chalk dust might've found its way into your bowl.'

I'd wished many times it could've been arsenic.

'As for the endless beatings on my ass with that wooden spoon? I have a tattoo of your most precious possession, those stupid orchids, on both butt cheeks so every time I sit down I know I'm squashing them.'

Childish, maybe, but those flowers had been my first tattoo and it'd made me feel so good I'd wanted more.

'I knew you would've hated the tattoos so every time I got another one, it was a real up yours.' I flipped the bird at the plaque, getting into the spirit of things. 'Whenever I lay in that parlour, the needle piercing my skin, I thought of how you'd rant and rave and disapprove, and I didn't feel a thing.'

On a roll, I continued. 'I hate you for destroying my trust in people. For making me believe I was unworthy. For making me feel I wasn't good enough for anything or anybody. But you know what? I'm doing okay. In fact, I'm doing better than okay. And Remy's a good guy. The best. So I guess I can be thankful you didn't screw him up real good too. We're happy. And that's the best form of revenge I know, because you're down there and there isn't one damn thing you can do to me any more...'

I trailed off, my legs surprisingly weak and my arms almost numb, like I was on the verge of fainting. I sank to my haunches, dropped my head and breathed deeply, in and out, until the dizziness passed.

He deserved so much more vitriol, but I felt drained and I couldn't summon any more hatred.

I was done.

Did I feel better? Maybe. Purging the past could only be a good thing.

But I wouldn't come back here. I'd said all that needed to be said. Who knew? Maybe I'd have the balls to confront Abby too now, and give her the closure she needed. It was the least I could do.

Not tonight. Tonight, I needed to head back to the club, immerse myself in work and finish that aged whiskey I'd been keeping for a rainy day.

The way I was feeling right now, it was pelting down.

I stood, staring at the plaque one last time. 'See you in hell.'

I walked away without looking back.

CHAPTER TWENTY-SEVEN

Abby

I FELT LIKE an idiot.

Getting tizzied up in a black miniskirt, green halter-top and stiletto ankle boots, with a liberal dose of mascara and coral lipstick, when Tanner had seen me naked.

But the clothes and make-up gave me some much-needed confidence as I strode towards the VIP rope inside Embue.

'I need to see Tanner King,' I said in my best diva voice, to a muscle-bound ninja who glared at me like I had no right being there let alone demanding audience with his boss.

He cast a cursory glance at the electronic tablet in his hand before shooting me a dismissive sneer. 'You're not on the list.'

'The boss will want to see her,' a guy said from behind me, unclipping the rope and pushing aside the gold curtain. 'Come with me, Abby.'

'Uh, thanks.' I swept past the himbo and smiled at the tall blond guy who bore a startling resemblance to British hottie Tom Hiddleston. 'I don't think we've met?'

'Hudson Watt, manager at this den of iniquity.' He shook my hand. 'And Tanner's best mate, no matter if he tells you otherwise.'

'Nice to meet you,' I said, those damn butter-flies taking flight when we stopped outside Tanner's private room. 'You sure this will be okay? He's not busy?'

'Sweetheart, he needs to see you so bad he doesn't even know it.' With a boyish grin, Hudson knocked twice on the door, swiped a card against the digital lock and opened it.

While my hands shook, he stuck his head around the door. 'You have a visitor.'

Before I could second-guess my wisdom in show-ing up here unannounced, Hudson swung open the door and gave me a nudge inside.

'Good luck,' he murmured, soft enough only I could hear, as he shut the door.

Leaving me staring at Tanner like a gobsmacked doofus.

Any scintillating opening lines I might have re-hearsed on the way over fled as he advanced towards me. Shoulders set, neck muscles rigid with tension, massive glower slashing his brows.

He didn't look pleased to see me.

I managed a pathetic 'hey' a second before he grabbed me and slammed his mouth against mine.

I could've protested, could've cited the fact we needed to talk, could've accused him of being a gut-less jerk for walking away from me without saying goodbye.

But as his tongue entered my mouth and he pinned me up against the door, any fleeting thought of resistance fled.

I wanted this. Wanted him. Like I'd never wanted anything in my life.

Lust consumed me as he unzipped, sheathed and rucked up my skirt. I clung to him, overwhelmed by sensation as he dragged my panties aside and thrust into me.

I gasped as he filled me, savouring the exquisite friction as he slid in and out. Slowly at first. Then faster. Each time he entered me harder than the last. Powerful thrusts. Pushing me higher, quicker, than I'd ever experienced before.

I hooked a leg over his waist and he took it as an invitation to pick me up, holding my butt as he drove into me like a man possessed.

My head fell back against the door with a thud as my muscles tensed, pleasure rippling through me as he angled my hips so he dragged across the most sensitive part of me.

With every thrust my body sparked with heat, burning me up as the beginnings of my orgasm pooled deep.

Long, deep, hard thrusts that made me want to bite down on something to stop from deafening him. He shifted. Drove into me again. Once. Twice. And I came apart, spiralling out of control as he swallowed my scream with a kiss.

He followed a moment later, thrusting into me so deep I almost passed out with the pleasure bordering on pain, his low groan fierce and feral.

Before I could say something light to defuse the

moment, he withdrew, leaving me no option but to lower my legs. He didn't look at me as he stalked to the bathroom, returning a moment later to sit at his desk like nothing had happened.

Reeling from his coldness, I tidied myself up and crossed the room to stand in front of him.

'Look at me.'

He ignored my demand, preferring to stare at a computer screen like it revealed the secret to longevity.

'Damn you.' I slammed my palm on his desk and he jumped, his gaze finally locking on mine.

What I saw took my breath away.

Disgust. Regret. And a hopelessness that made me want to cradle him close and never let go.

His throat convulsed as he swallowed, before clearing it. 'You need to leave.'

'Too bad, because I'm not like you, taking the easy way out, running away like some scared little kid.' I perched on his desk, close enough I could smell the alcohol on his breath. 'You don't look drunk but you smell like a brewery.'

'I'm not. I've had four shots.'

'To numb the pain?'

'To wake me up so I can work all night.' He faked a yawn and stretched, his deep scowl and defiant glare reminding me of a guarded lion taunting his prey before he pounced. 'You're disturbing me.'

'And you're disturbing me with this stupid act.' I jerked a thumb at the door. 'I'd like to think what just happened back there was you unable to keep your hands off me, but I think it was more about you proving a point.'

Fear lit his eyes before he glanced away. 'You don't
know what you're talking about. I'm a horny guy.
You're a babe. We burn up the sheets. Seemed like
you came here for one last fuck, so I obliged.'

Clamping down on the burgeoning hurt making
my chest ache, I mustered a sneer. 'If you're trying
to shock me into walking out of here, think again.'

I leaned forward, getting into his face. 'I'm onto
you.'

He pushed back from the desk and stood, putting
some distance between us. 'Look, you knew the type
of guy I was right from the start. I don't do emotion. I
don't do commitment. And I certainly don't do anything past its expiration date.'

He whirled back to face me, anger bracketing his
mouth. 'Remy came back, we were finished, so I made
it easy on the both of us. No drawn-out goodbyes. No
empty promises to stay friends.' He made a chopping
motion. 'A swift break.'

'So you did me a favour and I should be thanking
you?' I slow-handclapped as I stood and advanced towards him, projecting an outer calm when inside I was
a seething mess of wrath. 'Bravo. Thanks for taking
something special and tainting it with your asshat be-
haviour.'

Surprise widened his eyes imperceptibly before
the nonchalant mask slid back into place. 'We had
phenomenal sex, babe. Nothing special about that.'

'You're full of crap.' I laughed, a harsh sound devoid of amusement, while I resisted the urge to slap
him silly. 'Want to know what I think?'

'No,' he snapped, his lips compressing into a thin

line as he feigned boredom, glancing around the room at anything but me. Coward.

'You like to hide behind that bad-boy façade but inside you're so soft you're practically a marshmallow.'

Okay, so it lacked the delivery I'd envisaged in my head but at least it got his attention as he resumed glaring at me again.

'I bet you got those tattoos as part of your quest to be the bad boy, because that's what you believed you were.' I softened my tone as his jaw clenched, wanting to prod him into a reaction but unsure how far to push. 'But you're not bad, Tanner. You could never be bad and I'd like to stick around awhile and prove that to you.'

'Already told you, I've got work to do,' he said, deliberately misinterpreting what I meant.

'Don't do that, make me feel more stupid than I already do for coming here and laying myself open to you.' My voice cracked a little as my bravado faded.

What if I'd misread our relationship entirely?

It took less than two seconds for his expression to crumple and, relieved, I mentally yelled 'hallelujah'. A breakthrough.

'I'm sorry,' he said, leaning against the back of the sofa, swiping a hand across his face. 'I'm a shit.'

'You're a guy out of his comfort zone.' I perched next to him but didn't touch him, no matter how badly I wanted to. 'But I promise to be gentle with you.'

He flinched like I'd struck him. 'Unlike me. Fuck, I can't believe I took you like a madman before. And you were right. It was to drive you away once and for all. To show you what a prick I really am. But I forgot about the part where I can't get enough of you and...I went nuts. I'm sorry.'

'Do you hear me complaining?'

This time, I risked placing a hand on his forearm. He startled and shrugged it off, like I'd electrocuted him.

'You deserve so much better than me. Can't you see that?' He turned towards me, bleakness darkening his eyes to ebony. 'I'm no good for you.'

'I've spent my entire life having other people make decisions for me and pretending I'm okay with it. No more.' I snagged his hand, holding on tight when he tried to snatch it away. 'Don't you get it? You can't push me away no matter how hard you try. I like you, Tanner King.'

My chest tightened with the magnitude of what I had to say but if I didn't get the words out now, I never would. 'I may even be falling in love with you and if there's one thing I learned over the last year it's to fight for what I want.'

He didn't bolt at the L word, which I took as a good sign. What *wasn't* a good sign was the way all colour drained from his face and for a moment I thought he'd pass out.

'You don't mean that—'

'Stop telling me what to think or say or do.' I squeezed his hand, wishing I could infuse some of my belief into him. 'I'll put up with a lot but not that. Never that.'

I could see the war he waged as every conflicting emotion flickered across his face. Hope with hopelessness. Belief with disbelief. Incredulity with incredible, heart-warming anticipation.

I recognised them because I'd fought the same war over the last few days, but I'd come out on the other side, determined to be a victor.

'You're heading back to your old life. Your family. I'll only drag you down.' He sounded desperate, plucking at any excuse to keep us apart. It meant nothing. I'd faced harsher artillery from the Prendigast firing squad and come out on top.

'If you're going to eavesdrop, make sure you do it properly,' I said. 'I don't trust my family. I'm staying at Remy's.' I leaned closer so he couldn't misunderstand. 'I'm not going anywhere.'

He didn't speak for a long time after that and I let him process.

It had taken me three days to get to this point and even then I probably wouldn't be here if it weren't for Makayla's pep talk.

'I don't think I can be the man you want,' he whispered, sounding so bereft that something inside me shattered.

I knew what I said next could ultimately make or break us so I chose my words carefully, willing him to see the real me, willing him to believe.

'Why? Because you've never had a real relationship? Because you don't trust easily? Because your upbringing mucked you up so badly you don't think you're good enough?'

I slid to the floor, kneeling in front of him, hanging onto both his hands for dear life, imploring him to listen.

'We've both got trust issues. Hell, I didn't trust myself for so many years I can barely trust anyone else. But you showed me differently.' I gripped his hands tighter. 'You think I used you to get over my past? Maybe that was true at the start. But somewhere along the way I changed. Because *you* changed me.'

Emotion tightened my vocal cords and I swallowed to ease the dryness. 'I'm not ready to walk away from us, Tanner. What about you?'

Staring into his eyes was like staring into a fathomless dark pool. I couldn't read what he was feeling. Maybe it was nothing. I hoped it was everything.

When his grasp on my hands tightened, hope sprang to life. He stood and drew me to my feet until we were toe to toe, only the barest whisper of a breath separating us.

'How do I begin to make you understand how fucked up I am?'

Of all the things I'd envisaged him saying, that wasn't it. But I remained silent, hoping he'd continue.

'I want to believe you, Abby. I want to believe in us. But what if we're not enough?' His ragged breathing hitched. 'What if *I'm* not enough?'

I waited, sensing he wasn't finished, not by a long shot. My throat tightened and my eyes stung with unshed tears but I didn't speak, fervently wishing that whatever he had to say would allow us to move forward, together.

'I haven't told anyone this, not even Remy...' He sounded so morose, so heartbroken, I almost told him to stop. But his eyes had glazed, as if lost in painful memories, and I knew he had to purge whatever was bugging him if we were to have any chance. 'My dad hated me. From the time I was old enough to understand, probably around four, I felt it. Like he couldn't stand the sight of me.' Pain darkened his eyes and he blinked slowly, like waking from a coma. 'He did a good job of masking it when Mum or Remy were around, but if was just the two of us…man, the guy was a prick.'

My heart ached for what Tanner had gone through as a kid. My dad might have messed with my head, but at least he'd liked me. He'd never been deliberately cruel or condescending. He'd just expected me to do whatever he said and I'd been the idiot to put up with it.

'As I grew older, I could tell Mum couldn't stand him either and she was putting on a brave face for Remy and me. We'd spend all our time with her, even when he was home. She was probably protecting us but I didn't know it at the time…'

He dragged in a deep breath, released it. 'The day she died Remy was out, I was in the backyard and I heard them arguing inside. I got scared because Mum never shouted, and she was yelling so loud I thought the neighbours would hear. So I snuck up onto the veranda and hid outside the back door.'

A deep frown slashed his brows as he continued. 'Dad was saying some pretty horrific things. Flinging accusations like Mum had been having affairs and that she'd never loved him. Then he got to the good stuff…'

His expression contorted with grief and it took every ounce of my willpower not to haul him into my arms and tell him to stop. But if I did that, he'd clam up and I couldn't risk it. He'd come this far and if he hadn't divulged his secret to anyone before… well, I just hoped it indicated he trusted me and we had a shot in hell at a future once the truth came out.

'Apparently he'd fallen out of love with her since

Remy was born but he stuck around for four years. Then when he was going to leave her, she announced she was pregnant with me. He accused her of doing it deliberately, to trap him. And he hated me ever since, blaming me for trapping him in a marriage he didn't want. He would've walked away but child support payments for two kids would've crippled him financially so he stayed and made our lives a misery. Mum fired back, telling him to stay away from Remy and me and keep his hatred to himself. So he called her some pretty shocking names and Mum stormed out. Probably needed some time to cool down, so she went for a drive…'

He shook his head, agony twisting his mouth. 'She never should've driven in that state and ended up crashing into a tree not far from home.'

My throat ached with emotion and I touched his arm, trying to convey my sympathy, knowing it would be inadequate.

'Rather than comforting me after Mum died, you know what the bastard did? He blamed me. *Me*. For making him resentful and bitter, for making Mum have to defend me that day and ultimately being mad enough to have that accident that killed her. Blamed me for trapping him even more, since he'd be saddled with two kids he didn't want. I was ten fucking years old and he lumped all that on me. And it just got worse from there. For the next five years until he died, he treated me like shit. Never in front of Remy, who wasn't around much, but he made me feel worthless and useless, drumming it into me 'til I started to believe it… I cried with joy the day he died. Remy put up with my teenage tantrums for the next few years and I bided my time 'til I hit eighteen and had access to my trust fund to start my life. These?' He brandished his tattoo-covered arms at me. 'Getting inked ensured I was reborn. I was never comfortable in my old skin, so I took on a new one. One guaranteed to keep people at bay, which suited me fine. In a screwed-up way, I identified with my dad, not wanting to ever be trapped in a relationship. So I never let anyone get close. Until you…'

His tortured gaze met mine and I held my breath, silently praying we'd had a breakthrough and that he wouldn't send me packing once and for all.

'You saw beneath my tats.' My chest ached with the effort of holding back a torrent of emotion. When he cupped my face, the breath I'd been holding seeped out in an embarrassing squeak. 'You really see me, the real me…and I don't know whether to hold onto you for ever or run as fast as I possibly can without looking back.'

Hope flared to life but I forced myself to stand still as he released my face, to lower his hands to my hips. He hadn't pushed me away. He hadn't bolted. Yet.

So I tried to convey my sorrow at his atrocious upbringing, knowing I'd come up short but having to try regardless.

'Sorry is so trite now but, Tanner, I can't begin to tell you how sorry I am for what you went through. You shouldered a burden you shouldn't have and were raised by a sadist. Just know that I do see you. And I always will.'

I couldn't hold back the tears, not any more, so I let them fall, wrapping my arms so tight around him he yelped.

The good thing was, he held me too, burying his nose in my hair like he used to do.

The bad thing was, once I started crying, I couldn't stop. It was like all the feelings I'd bottled up for so long came tumbling out in a torrent. He held me until the sobs subsided, strong and stoic, the man I wanted, the man I needed.

When I finally eased away, I glimpsed the first flicker of a smile and my heart soared.

'And you had the audacity to call me a marshmallow?' He kissed the tip of my nose and I knew we'd marched out of the front lines, together. 'You're just a big cry-baby.'

I punched him in the chest. 'But I'm your cry-baby.'

'I guess you are.' He didn't hesitate and joy fizzed in my veins. 'For some inexplicable reason, you see the best in me. You bring out the best in me. And I want to see how far this can go.'

I let out a whoop and he laughed, picking me up and swinging me around.

'But you need to promise me something,' he said, sounding serious.

'Anything.'

'If you're going to walk away at any stage, do me the courtesy of telling me.' He tightened his hold around my waist. 'I don't think I could handle being left hanging.'

'Like you did to me the last three days?'

He grimaced. 'Touché.'

I held up my right hand. 'I promise. Anything else?'

'I...I think I love you too,' he said, gruff and bashful.

'I said I like you.' Grinning, I slid my palms up

his chest to rest on his beautifully broad shoulders. 'Maybe I'm only halfway to loving you.'

Cockiness curled his upper lip. 'You love me. You're just too stubborn to admit it.'

Joy made me cling to him, like I'd float away if I blinked and realised this was a dream. 'Maybe you'll have to kiss a confession out of me?'

'Too easy,' he murmured, a second before his mouth claimed mine.

His lips coaxed and tempted, demanding a response I was only too willing to give. A long, slow, soul-searing kiss that would be the first of many. A kiss filled with hope. A kiss to build a future on.

Reluctant to come up for air, I gently pushed him away.

'Okay, I'll admit it.' I pretend pouted. 'I love you. Happy?'

'Sweetheart, you have no idea how much.'

As he hugged me tight, the pounding of his heart matching mine, I had a fair idea.

Unconditional love.

There was no feeling in the world like it.

Now that I'd found it with this incredible, infuriating man, I had no intention of ever letting go.

*   *   *   *   *

LET'S TALK

Romance

For exclusive extracts, competitions
and special offers, find us online:

f facebook.com/millsandboon

◎ @millsandboonuk

🐦 @millsandboon

Or get in touch on 0844 844 1351*

For all the latest titles coming soon, visit
millsandboon.co.uk/nextmonth